there seemed a river

brian david cinadr

redwood publishing, llc
ladera ranch, ca

for more information, contact redwood publishing at:
info@redwoodpublishing.com

printed in the united States of america

isbn 978-1-947341-85-2 (paperback)
isbn 978-1-947341-86-9 (ebook)

library of congress control number: 2019918829

https://briandavidcinadr.com/

for her it seemed and in the end, for him, for all we've lost

1

the road followed the river and the river to the coven of a great lake, something the water had known all along, the instinct of a rain and roads go home. i hadn't seen another car for almost an hour, since the highway and just the lights of the lonesome gas station town half way. there were no stars, out here only head-lights could burn, out here on this edge at the ragged ends of a middle and a midwest. i pushed my tongue between my teeth until it hurt and satisfied somehow, turned the air conditioning off and let the windows down and the night in, the rental car plastic out into the trees. i looked at my eyes in the rear view mirror rather than behind me, there was only black behind me, i knew damn well where i'd been. i pushed the radio knob until it clicked off and thought how everything is digital now and never dials and listened to the nothing of everything around me.

the night rattled in the backseat, in my chest, between my ribs and the stories there, forty years before this. i stopped the car and opened the door, the car dinging some engineered electric sound. i only got out to piss, but the air filled up my arms and something not of the air, but of the earth, some rich dirt secret, rain and bones and animal oil. the trees came and went against the boils of heat lightning, everything else only indigo outside the insect catch of the car lights. i'd crossed the river, the bridge stones in the taillights' light behind me. this is my land, my family's land and their dust, the line between here and there and i was here where i'd always been no matter how far. the river was there below me, its hum in the air between the trees and years, something breathed in and never out. it was alive in me as sure as blood, the old man inside my limp, my crepe paper mother.

the trees here grow down from the sky almost to the clay. their roots the truth after all, gasps into the river's edge where the river has ate the earth away until they've told too much and lose their hold and fall. i got back in the car, the night seemed to follow me. i pulled back on the tar stuck tarmac and then off to the right about a mile down and onto our road and another bridge, the pop and griddle of the gravel under the wheels and the old house there.

this is the beginning and the end, the house i was raised in, a straight tooth on an uneven jaw. it is a flatboard house on a rise of land banked above the high water mark my grandfather remembered in red paint. i never knew him, i only knew his slightly crooked '36 on the near bridge and the straight line he drew beneath it, a quiet photo of him squinting in the sun like he never looked any different. it was the only house for a mile by memory, a sturdy ghost in the sweep of the car's headlights, white wash like it should, still solid and two stories and as high as it is wide, proportions that somehow made it seem worthy if not beautiful and pitch roofed and windowed and four steps up to a wood porch, something squared and not three.

the key's still above the back door, the smell of the house and the old wood around me like it never left me, candles and matches and the metal flashlight you have to shake to make work in the same left kitchen drawer. everything is like it's always been, she's lived here so long she doesn't know where anything is anymore. the old man knew, but the old man is dead, like jesus dead and door nailed and never coming back, his body at kapelka's mortuary, that much she knows. he died this early morning, the end of a wednesday's work and finally some rest, i guess. this land under his fingernails like he never left.

she said he died in his sleep, three tries at a last breath, his hand run down her back and all a life just over like that, a whole life, his life and part of mine and hers. and if the little lord's prayer lets her sleep now, let her. he picked the yellow cooking apples to eat, and maybe she liked pink ladies, but she ate the yellow apples anyway, so let her do what she wants to now.

what happened here, happened between us, between the rain and the darkness and the disquiet of the silence after. it rained all summer and eighteen years maybe, it's hard to remember, i can only remember now. my memory unraveling from my spine like a loose string, like something i need and can't use. and everything i know has worn threadbare from the years and the miles. and everything i remember is black and white or an acid color instamatic '72 or '68, the date in a white frame around what has turned into my memory. a childhood faded to a few snap shots, her and him, what became the two of them, standing in front of the house like flag poles, a christmas or an early easter sunday. i would lose everything that year, this last year, everything that i thought was mine, i'd barely borrowed for a time and time itself is a lie. all my life like a storm i was caught in, but the rain i could never keep.

she's in there in the downstairs bedroom now, in the middle of the bed, just the sound of her breathing like the river, what you can't hear when you listen, what you notice when it stops. the night is in the house, the windows open, the dim kitchen light and a dimmer flicker from her room, candles lit, the smell of paraffin and prayers. she's in the persimmon of a damp sleep, a density of dreams all about her petty head. her chest barely rises and falls, little lifes and deaths, lifes and deaths. i watch, waiting for the next tide and think about my own air, counting to myself as i walk into the musk of the dark house, into the moth draw of the kitchen. my skin a sepia, some shade of yellow or brown reflected in the greasy windows looking out, something of then, something of him and her and the quiet we were wove in, the house around us like a secret we all knew and never told. i turn the kitchen light off, click, lick my fingers and pinch the candle flames closed, climbing the hopeless stairs in the dark to my childhood room as if any light would be too much. the old mattress springs rust and barely resist my immortal weight, my body like a great lake, too heavy to move, in place now after the glacier.

i pray i'll sleep and for a sun to come to burn all my prayers away, all these pin prick memories in my head, leave me to pick up lucky pennies instead, cash money i could have saved, small moments of matter and consequence i should remember, i've forgotten already. and everything is a moonless sky and the river's hush and an impossible heat and not even summer.

2

the sun has started with a whip crack, i sit up still in my clothes, the bed so small my feet hang over the end. everything is first morning golden and green thru the veins of limbs and new leaves, the dark pushed into the ground and to the corners of the room. i know where i am, but i don't know who i am, i'm happy for a moment, before i open my eyes wide, but the truth has its way like water in the cracks, no daybreak is going to break this yolk of sadness. my shadow hangs on the floor at my ankles. i left my boots under the bed, my feet strange on the stairs, too big to walk straight down.

i think it's cool outside, it's hot in here. the house is still, stifled, the air used up and old. my father ran the fan at night, sometimes in the winter with the window closed if he couldn't sleep. she was always cold, even in july.

she's sleeping in the spare bedroom downstairs. i knock on her open door for nothing else to say. her eyes are already open, but she doesn't seem awake like she's still looking into her sleep.

"mom?"

"you're home, i didn't even hear you last night, did you sleep in our room?"

"no, mom i slept in my old room."

"but there's no bedding, there's not room for the two of you."

"it's fine, mom."

"i didn't want you to sleep in that old bed, i washed the bedding in our room, it's all clean."

"mom, dad just died in that bed, i'm not sleeping in there."

"where did nicole sleep?"

"nik didn't make the trip."

"i just cleaned the bedding."

"why aren't you sleeping in there?"

"i sleep here now, i don't like the fan."

"the fan's just in the window, you don't have to turn it on if you don't want to."

"mom, it's too hot upstairs not to turn the fan on."

"anyway, you'll be more comfortable in there, i just washed everything."

"mom, i'm not going to sleep in your bed, okay?"

"but everything is ready for you."

she's still talking, almost to herself or to god or the ghosts she sees, as i make my way back up the stairs. the thought of sleeping in their bed setting in my head like a hornets' nest and between my shoulder blades and yet i can't help but to stop at the door of their room. i look in at the space where my father had slept, the same as i might slow down by a highway accident and try not to stare. the room is dark, their room was always dark, i have no memory of a sunlight there, the windows shrouded with a puzzle of trees and north facing. i thought that i might feel something, some sense of him, but the only wraith dragging thru the hall is me and my kid memories. everything around me is just the same so i don't have to remember. all his things are there, their bedroom like before, his heavy pants hung over the chair, rain boots by the door, his slicker and a pair of worn shoes he won't wear anymore purposely on a stack of magazines, a futile lamp he probably found and tried to fix, his glasses sad on the dresser, what he saw the world thru and just plastic now and polished glass and useless to see his way into this death.

i feel my way back to my room, i put my boots on and feel more myself, tied tight and right on my feet. it's strange to be a man in the house, the walls awkward and ill fitting like a thrift store suit, the smell of moth balls just above the decay. it was a house to be young in and just married, a charming starter that needed work, but it is only them and the teeth they had between them, twenty some years since i'd left. it is the old people's house you point to and still a surprise when you look inside. a house to wait day out and day in and sleep in dust and die in. drains narrowed with bits and pieces of them, hair and skin and sink drips that didn't matter enough to fix and rusted where they dripped and faucets that merely spit, a jilted fireplace crowded with soot, lights that groan out yellow bones or sit darkly silent, '20's wiring and rotten bulbs, a bulb broken off in the socket. all the universe is falling from its big bang center and stone walls fall to just stones, along the back where they once held off the hill. and even the wallpaper is only waiting for her to die now and the relief of white paint.

"there's not much for breakfast."

she shuffles where she used to walk, lighting candles for prayers like a musty nun, her spine bent like a field weed, a queen anne's lace, well past flowered and gone to straw.

"i'll just have tea, mom, i can eat in town, is bob's still there?"
"you can make toast."
"what about bob's, mom?"
"bob boras is dead, god rest his soul, i think your father had some coffee around here."

"this bread's all moldy, mom, there has to be somewhere to eat in town."

"his daughter carol anne took over, you remember carol anne, she's so thin i think she does drugs with that group down at the townhouse tavern, richie zak and all of them."

"mom, i don't care about all that, i just need to eat breakfast, okay."

"you remember carol anne, it's a shame, she has two children that are just darling, her husband left her, he lives in canada or kentucky somewhere."

"i just want to get something to eat and see dad, are you coming with me?"

"i see her mother at church, she always asks about you."

"mom, are you going to get ready?"

"she never mentions him, i think it was another woman."

"mom, please just get ready so we can go."

"i'm going to stay home, john kapelka's taking your father for the cremation first thing this morning and i don't want to have to rush... here's the coffee."

"when did you decide to cremate dad?"

"i don't want to rush this morning."

"did dad want to be cremated?"

"i want your father cremated."

"why didn't you tell me?"

"james david, your father's at peace now … and i'm at peace, everything's arranged."

"call the mortuary and tell them not to touch dad until i see him."

"your father and i talked all about this."
"just call them, mom! i have to see him, i haven't seen him in..."

i feel a burn start in the back of my throat, a cistern of tears i keep and won't cry. i feel for my keys in my pocket without any luck, the whole weight of this house and her and the fat of a past pressing down on me. i don't remember leaving, just the screen door slamming behind me so i know i'm outside, out the back door and into the thick air and the familiar smell of the old man's mercury to save me, his truck too old and rust and rotting away behind the shed. it's just morning and it's hot already, too hot not to rain.

"do you want this coffee, i made instant coffee."

her crooked frame holding a cracked cup at the back porch half in and half out the door.

"i don't drink coffee! just call the mortuary and tell them to wait!"

the car starts and i let the engine roar as i utter "you crazy bitch" to myself and the wheels on the gravel again and finally the road along the river and something that makes sense.

3

there's a certain refuge to a road, a place to be even if you don't know where you're going, but i know where i'm going, i was born and raised here. there's just one way to town and to the lake, like a heartache or a peninsula, you have no choice. the road and the river were all i knew as a kid and so much bigger then than the whole world now. riding into town in the old man's truck, me in the middle if she went, but she hardly ever went, always asking if he'd taken a shower or what "stinking samples" was he taking today, and saying no then, and staying home or taking her car towards the highway and the riddle-me-ree of an east unknown to me. i never cared, i hated her, her bent over voice and her medicine face, her drug store perfume like a scary dream i couldn't quite remember or shake. my father smelled of work and cigarettes, whiskey and earth, the vague tin of the river, bits and pieces of the

creation he collected and took to town and mailed to the
university. i'd sit with the samples between my rubber kid
legs and he'd nod down at them and say, "there's a whole
world in there as big as ours." and i'd look in like a god
that can only kill and look out the window like i might
be staring out of a jar and watch the rain run along the
glass and look up at the sky brooding thru the trees, their
skeletons in winter, and watch the tar and the gravel blur
by and shards of the river and imagine i was running next
to the truck.

"how fast are we going, dad?"
"48 ... i've never gone faster."

i crank the window open and lean across the breadth of
the merc's big bench seat and roll the other window down
until it sticks three quarters of the way, never letting up
on the accelerator or myself. the air is a tapestry, a luxury of spring and almost a skin. every breath burdened
with green smells and a muddy childhood and always the
chance of rain, an old vinyl smell that still rings in the car
and all these thoughts and the river won't stop and the
engine missing maybe, but still pressing me down the road.

"fuck."

i say it to myself, but out loud with all my breath as if i

expect an answer and letting the air back into my lungs while i wait.

"you'll get thru this ... god, get me thru this."

it's not a prayer, it's a plea, the need to hear a voice other than my mother's in my head, trying to remember my father's voice, and nikki's tiny wire voice two nights before. the same phone conversation i've had at the end of every girl, 2 am, a broken bottle sorry too late again and unforgiven and never forgotten, her death rattle, "i'll always love you" and finally someone says "well maybe someday" and then you both know it's over. it was over months ago. i went back to bed, but i wouldn't sleep. the old man would die hours later while i laid awake breathing. i called her as soon as i hung up with my mother. i had no one else to call at 5 am. she said she was there for me because there was nothing else she could say. we both knew it was a lie, but i believe in lies, i was raised on them.

i first saw her on the church of a sidewalk, an uncommon sun above her, better than the streetlight halos i was used to, a tuesday's last shadows half way across the street. she was beautiful then, more beautiful now and something of the bay air, a rain before it touches the ground, a san francisco and all the magic of a north beach corner, grant and vallejo and the trieste making italian coffee and me with a cup of tea. she sat at the table next to me absently spooning foam from a latte into a renaissance mouth and reading the lover thru her glasses. i asked if she liked it, she said yes before she looked up and yes again when our eyes met, they were green, maybe blue. she asked me if i'd ever read duras, i told her i read plath instead. i didn't tell her i meant the latte. i slid across the bench seat along the window to her table like i might know her forever and she closed her book, her book mark still on the table and sat back against the glass and an east sky. the light was just off her, just after the sun and everything was dying into night and everything was newborn pink and blue and everything around her was about her and she didn't even know.

i said james, she said nikki, but she hesitated, i wondered if she meant to say nicole. i asked her where her accent was from, she said she had lived all over europe and australia, that she was born in switzerland, but she barely remembers, that she lives here now, but she doesn't know why. we talked about this big america and the old man italians drinking espressos under their caps and hats and the street lamp. we talked about ghosts and midwest towns as if there was a difference and her little idea about mexico. she took her glasses off and ran her fingers thru her hair, i decided to lean my chin on my hand. we watched all the sidewalk peoples tatter by, looking down or at themselves in the windows and smoking or just breathing and listened to the coffee house talk, poems shot out from drunks like new gospels, news accounts from poets. we sat until even the trieste closed and i would walk her home to the top of jones, into the fog like she lived in the sky.

i wouldn't see her for a week, but i'd see her the next friday and every day after and time stopped and wouldn't start again until i opened my eyes again. it was a lock of life, of evenings inside her light and the light of the burned down candles she lit with a long match as she went around the room like a bright planet. she made deep pans of lasagna and french stews wove with turnips and provincial spells. i brought cheap bottles of red we finished on the fire escape after dinner, stars or satellites maybe, above her and all around her head. i couldn't recognize the city without her now, all it's crooked teeth up and down the hills and painted colors and sounds, everything starting and stop-ping and never really stopping, not really.

we spent days in washington square huddled in the sun and on the sunny sides of the sidewalk, sitting with all the old chinese snug in quilted coats and their paper east, bending and swaying in the breeze like trees, tai chi in the heart of this little italy, peter and paul cathedral ringing. and the nights went on, neon and mercury vapor, and everything started up a careless columbus and down a broadway like an idea that spread, a jazz marmalade played out into the street, a warning of luck in the yellow belly of the chinatown, dice in the back, mysterious meals in the front, obvious plates of pasta at sodini's, where else. the two of us rang out in the sound of everything, faces and the fog horn and the stockton bus brrr, the cable car's cable whirs under the street like the blood of the city, the pity of the bay on us all, our dirty waters running below our feet and to the cheap ocean waiting.

and when it was time we went up the hill home, up the old stone stairs that ran thru her crazy building like a fault. the morning of her keys and the earth of the big wood door, the city behind us and lock it twice, the handle and the bolt. whispers and a warm mouth, legs a long prayer god must have uttered to himself, the two of us tying ourselves into a knot under the rain's soft psalm on the roof and the milk sky above that, above the sidewalk and the street. second stories and second chances that aren't always quite so clement, the two of us chance characters sleeping a child's happy sleep. we were sinful and beautifully unknowing, dreaming in the dreamless black of lust and love, tangled in one another like twigs. and one night i woke to the crash of her skin in the moonlight in the window or the street light maybe, and my heart broke at the curve of her hip, a bend i could never make or live up to. and i knew right then i was born to love her and secretly hurt her and drive her away because i always knew she would leave.

i'm on the road for now and i'm nearly happy if not desperate, reckless just to get away from the city, from the
old house and my mother's toy head. i'm agitated or even
curious to see my father's dead body, but death owns a
peculiar excitement over us we can only live thru to know.
there's no cell signal this side of the highway, a hundred
miles of hope that nik's called and left me a message, but
i put off checking at the house. it's always better to hope
than to know.

there are more houses now as i near town, bigger vacation
houses between the old towny houses that have always
been here, back behind the trees, just ideas as i drive by.
the fuel gauge's needle is almost laying on empty. i know
the old man always kept enough gas to get to town.

"what the fuck?"

a black cadillac hearse passes by me heading east, a long
darkness behind it.

"holy fucking shit, you've got to be fucking kidding me."
i'm talking to myself, somehow things make more sense
out loud, an only child, my voice has always been "us". i
put the brake to the floor, the merc heaves like a broken
herd animal and pulls to the right into the gravel and mud.

"fuck."

i know if i don't get back on the road i'll be up to the axles in the soft shoulder, stuck. i jerk the wheel to the left, the car too heavy to roll skips sideways across both lanes and finally exhausted of inertia and a hub cap, comes to a stop inches from another car in the opposite lane.

"fuck."

everything has stopped, only the earth spinning and a hub cap rolling into the woods, but i can't notice. there's an old couple in some midsize sensible car staring wide eyed at me in the middle of the road.

"fuck off!"

they seem surprised. i glare at them like van gogh mad in some french field and peel away, the engine old and almost ridiculous, but of an age of brute horsepower still. a tack of blue burnt oil and spoiled gasoline fills the car and everything behind me. i turn back after the hearse, the wheel is pulling hard to the right, the front end of the merc crippled with mishap, the entire car wobbling at 65. there's no way to drive faster than 50, there's no way to know how much further the merc has until it runs empty, but any reason stopped two days ago. the engine is at the edge of disaster, i'm leaning forward like my english might push the car faster, my foot to the floor, my hands choke the wheel trying to hold it steady as if this is the only moment of my life. i almost lose the road again around a curve, the brakes are filled with resentment and mud, soft and ineffective. i'm outside my head, i can't think, i'm purely physical, i can only react, unconscious and animal and close to perfect in this instant.

the hearse is up ahead now, in and out of the shadows and somehow darker than the rest of the road and the woods around it. i can see it in little dreams between the trees around the curves and then just in front of me like a morning. i come up hard on his rear, hit the horn, flash the lights, their reflection in the blacked out back window of the converted caddie. kapelka must have washed the hearse before he left, its black almost white in the breaks of light and a few runs of water down the back door like a washed apple. my father's cars were always filthy with the gravel road and mud and samples from the river. i wonder if it's strange for him to be in something so clean.

"what the fuck, this fucking guy isn't going to stop."

i actually look to my right as if there were someone there to react. i'm a foot from the hearse's bumper, i'm pounding on the horn, flashing the lights, nothing.

"you're pissing me off... you stupid fuck."

i whisper thru the windshield, more to myself, as i cross the double yellow line, it seems like a sin if not a last request, murder – suicide if there's anyone coming west, the mercury right up next to him now.

"pull over!"

i yell thru the wind of the open windows, waving my hand. i can see him behind my reflection in the darkened glass as the hearse accelerates ahead.

"god damn it! you fucking idiot! pull over!"

now i'm screaming out the window. i drive my boot down onto the gas pedal, i can hear it hit the floor and the engine's hesitant gulp of gasoline and air, a moment for regret, but it's too soon for any thought, the big eight's startling combustion pushes me past any rational. the merc slams into the back of the hearse, empty sample bottles come from under the merc's seats and gather around my feet and the passenger side floor. the hearse speeds up. i'm raging, i'm not in my head or my body, i'm only in my narrow sight like i'm staring thru a diamond. i am pure emotion, bone teeth and crimson, there is nothing to dilute me, i am only blood. i revel in the contact as i smash into his rear bumper again, but i stay on the accelerator pushing him into the muddy shoulder of the road.

i might be screaming. the mire finally grabbing his front
right wheel, the hearse slipping into a chaos, but it's long
and heavy and feigns capsizing until it finally stops buried
in the deep mud of an old rain.

i leave the merc running still in the road, the engine pains
and pings and hollers, the hearse's new motor just seems
to be breathing. i'm out of the car on the asphalt, the road
seems bigger on foot. i'm looking down at my boots so i
don't lose the earth and the gravity i take for granted and
then into the driver's side window of the hearse where
there's only my reflection and the mutt of trees and a
battered sky behind me. i can hear the river and the sound
of my breathing, the click of electric door locks.

4

i'm at the frayed ends of adrenaline, the breathless moment between a branch bending impossibly and it's snap, but we're all strongest at the point before we break. the air smells of fresh mud, a loom of brown and green, earth and sky, the portent of a rain hung on the northern, its siren raising up the lake. we're in a deep wood, but for the asphalt and its history of oil, there are only trees otherwise and the river somewhere. my voice cracks the eggshell of the silence, of motors running and the sound of everything we don't hear, a morning sound, even before the scrape of the sun, before anything, when there's only nothing, only locust waiting deep in the ground.

"i had to stop you, you have my father."

"get away!"

"i'm sorry, but i couldn't let you cremate him... before i see him."

"stay away from me, i'm calling the police."

his small voice is muffled by the glass, looking up at me from the mud spattered window like a bug. i immediately think of my father's samples and this little man's strange life of death.

"i'm james tully, you have my father in the car."

"i'm calling the police right now."

"just open the fucking door! ... i need to see my father."

he steps on the gas, his face is a knotted string, tied and untying, frantic, the hearse's back wheel spins burning rubber and sending mud up into the wheel well and onto the road, the car doesn't move, only sinking in deeper. i only speak when the wheel stops.

"i have to see him, i haven't seen him in ....."

 i'm embarrassed to say it's been twelve years.

"...twelve years... jesus."

i mutter to myself. i feel all my past rising up in my throat, too much to remember and forget. i spit out what i can, swallow hard on the rest. my words are thin and squeezed tight. my skin barely holds onto my bones. my arms rattle, my hands at their ends like loose change in a pant pocket.

"come on, please! just open the door and give me a few minutes to see him, please, i need to do this, i've... i've come a long way."
"you're crazy, you could have killed me, i'm calling the police."
"you're not calling the fucking police, there's no god damn cell signal out here anyway, so put your phone away and open the fucking door!"
"get away from this car, this is ... sacrilegious."
"this isn't a fucking church, it's a delivery service."
"that's not true, i'm not listening to you, you have no idea of my solemn duties."
"oh my god, solemn duties? you're a bad barber at best!"
"you're uninformed and… and you're profane."
"shut up."

i'm secretly proud that i didn't tell him to shut the fuck up. we both look towards the hiss of an approaching car, the old couple i almost hit miles back. she's driving, coming behind the mercury at a parade pace, both of them staring like dumbfounded owls.

"you're a menace!"

the old man shaking as he spits out the words with a righteous spirit, the old woman adding...

"we're calling the police."

she probably finishes all his sentences. all i can see of her are her boned hands on the wheel and her thick round glasses.

"help me! help! he tried to kill me!"

i turn to look at the little man, he and i are both shocked at his outburst. the old couple's faces smooth with panic, the old man rolling up the window as they speed around the mercury at 20 miles per hour, into the next curve and into the uncertainty of the trees. i look up like i might see a heaven, my hands on my head like this madness may be right. i turn away from the car window and start to laugh, the branch snapped. i walk down the side of the road in a disturbing calm, almost hysterical, drunken with the day and the night before and before that. i am the purity of exhaustion, empty of interpretation, fucked up and holy. i find a stone at the side of the road worn smooth from a million years of the river, it's just larger than my hand, it's weight is blameless and the only sure thing i know. i carry it over to the driver's side window of the hearse, my face only inches from his, but i'm looking at mine.

i'm forty, i have my father's pedestrian eyes, brown and worn like old shoes and maybe my mother's sharp nose. otherwise, i have nothing, only what i made myself, a shock of black hair receded back, black irish, a ravaged face strangely interesting maybe if not handsome, a solid celt jaw pressed into the moment. it seems years since i saw myself. the little man is probably my age, but he looks years older and colorless by this time. his skin wax thru the glass, his hair is brown or gray and not black and combed and combed over a balding spot on top and behind his head. he's the only person who can't see it. he has a mustache that someone might grow to feel serious, trimmed and offi-cious. he's squared, narrow shouldered. he's wearing the black suit that he wears everyday when he's not wearing the navy blue, a different white shirt than yesterday, a red tie the wife bought him for a holiday or his mother, he doesn't remember who, there's probably no difference. i knock on the window with the stone and smile.

"open the doors so i can see my father."

the little man only looks up at me sadly and even smaller, a bible school jesus at the last supper play. i drop the rock and turn and lean against the door, my back to him. i can feel the cool of the window glass thru my t-shirt.

"god, what am i doing? ... i quit."

i say it out to the air, i'm three thousand miles and two days past weary, the heat a bad thought i can't get out of my head. i want to lay down in the cool mud and sleep until i wake up. and maybe i can dream again, maybe, or stretch out on a big flat rock in the sun next to the river, feel the light burn red thru my eye lids, wade into the white shallows when it gets too hot, let the water run around me, let all my silt down to the bottom and come home with my pockets filled with fool's gold. the hearse locks click and break my daydream. i almost wish they hadn't.

i walk to the back of the hearse because i have to and open the double doors, there's a gurney and the outline of feet under a drastic sheet in front of me. there's a sanitary smell, plastic or chemical, and the good smell of a new car, i doubt my father ever rode in a new car. i'm standing in mud, my boots feel permanent in the ground, the only thing keeping me to the earth without the old man to root me. she was never there, she was out at church or in her bottle cotton head and never anything to me besides mother. and now nikki's gone and just an ache in my side where she was, a memory of the rib we shared, the rib she took with her and the dylan cds.

"he hasn't been prepared."

the little man is somehow next to me, up out of the ground like a mushroom.

"what?"

"your father, he's being cremated, he's not prepared for viewing."

"i... i need to see him, i haven't seen him in twelve years."

"give me a few minutes, please, i'll ready him as best i can, then you can spend some time with the deceased."

the little man is sweating, he had bacon and burnt toast for breakfast, his wife thinks he likes it that way because he eats it. he wears brut after shave, but not today. he climbs into the back of the hearse barely stooped over, he closes the doors behind him. i wait. if i smoked this is when i would light up, but i can only stare at my hands. my mind is searching for what to think, something, but there's nothing, the nothingness of death or nirvana maybe, but i'm not enlightened, i'm only empty and heavy with the moment, all of it turning to vinegar in my head.

there's an oily raven down the road picking at the jerk of some small murdered animal, a squirrel or a young raccoon run over. there's two more waiting on the wire above, their eyes are greasy and bottomless as if it all made sense. all of nature living out this circle, while we stutter and interpret and try to live out a line. all of us clouded with intellect and religion, searching for answers and time when the real order of life is water clear and lived out regardless of what we see. the little man opens the doors, i'm startled, the birds pay no attention. the musk of the

car and his clothes mix and mate and acid out the back
into the moss air, into my head so i know it will be all that
i remember, a smell of ammonia and burnt toast and brut
after shave just above the want of decay.

the little man is waiting for me to climb into the back, he
says nothing, but i know. he closes the doors behind me
almost shut. my father is facing me, gray almost blue, the
blue of deep veins and blood spent of oxygen. the sheet
has been folded down, the gurney raised, a papery hospital
gown up and around his chest. his hands are open like
unearthed roots and somehow magnificent, awkwardly
pressed together over him, his arms dead tree limbs, the
rest of him kindling. his mouth is open, his eyes are closed,
he is the husk of his rage and a residue of his quiet study,
a slide sample between thin plates of glass, a sample of
life, but not life. i'm reverent, nearly rapt with the detail
of his end, the lake of death we all run to, this part of me
complete. there's nothing of him left, his body an artless
sketch, uninspired and only accurate, but you can't see life
when it's living and the quietude of death only allows us a
close look at where we lived once and never why. he knew
that. samples were samples and never the river.

there's a crunch of car tires, an incantation of a two way
radio, the tick of a fan belt from a ford crown vic. the
sky has darkened so i can see the flash of lights thru the

hearse's windows on the little man's face. the heat inside the car is pressing in on me like i'm deep under water, my father's hands are ice cold, i'm crying, it was too hot not to rain. the storm is starting thru the trees, its water broke and run down the windows and on the car's metal roof. the rain's patter is all i'll remember, i'll never remember my voice or my broken words to him, what i'm only saying to myself. there's nothing of my father here, only what he left me and left me to live with. i can hear his voice almost in my chest, in the trees like ten thousand birds. i hear the little man's voice and a large voice, the kind of voice that comes from under a hat.

5

"kapelka, what the hell's goin' on here?"
"hello sheriff, um, it's the son of the deceased, sheriff."
"you're performin' wakes on the river road now?"
"he's being cremated, there was no viewing."
"don't shit me, we got a call from the highway patrol, says
some old timers called up at the gas station, said there
was a high speed chase and someone was getting killed."
"oh, it was just a mistake, i pulled too far off the road."
"what the hell happened to the back end there?"
"oh, that ... i backed into a grave stone last week, didn't
even see it, they're very difficult to see in the mirrors."
"are you shitting me, kapelka?"
"sheriff, i'm not .... everything is fine, i'm going to need
the tow truck, perhaps you could call up at the lake?"
"you're full of shit."

the doors of the hearse open, the nearing storm's air is new and almost cold, it fills into the hearse like a curse or the redemption of an old high school grudge. the sheriff is bow legged, long necked and bone stuck shoulders. he's thin, but he has a belly, something he's satisfied with and rubs after big meat and flour dinners and sunday church brunches. he's under a wide brimmed hat and sun glasses he's worn for 15 years, surely. his face is a dog-eared book of western dreams or a yellowed machine manual.

"and what's your story?"
"what?"
"what's your name?"
"i'm james tully, officer."
"sheriff! take off your hat, you're in the presence of the deceased."

the little man seems taller, upright with the lord. the sheriff clumsily takes off his glasses and his hat, its shape matted into his hair. he is ordinary without them, thin nosed and almost frail.

"sorry ... all right, well, let's get this mess taken care of then, i need to get that old merc off the road and we'll get you out of here and back on towards the highway."

i step down out of the hearse, the mercury is quiet and likely out of gas. the little man is back into the car attending to the body, i only look back to see him drape the sheet over my father's face. i'll never see him again.

the sheriff is in the cruiser on the radio, his hat back on, his sun glasses hanging on his shirt pocket opposite his badge. the air is sharp with the bleach of rain, but we're just at the edge of the storm and the start. the sky is yellow and black. the sheriff steps out of his car looking up at the clouds, the rain about him, starting and stopping, ghosts of water and the heat up off the asphalt.

"god damn rain, rained near everyday for three weeks i think, the damn river's gonna bust her sides this keeps up."
"yeah, it seems pretty wet."

we're talking about the weather, people always wind up talking about the weather, only discussing what they can't change.

"let's get this car off the road before someone gets killed, come on kapelka you can help push!"

the little man puts his head out the hearse's door a shy rodent.

"i've got it."

i open the car door, put the merc in neutral, my feet outside the car, i lean into the steering wheel, the car starts forward, my breath held and suddenly the car moves ahead, the sheriff behind pushing on the bumper, his boots scraping on the just wet asphalt.

"steer it over, boy."

i turn the wheel and try to push again, the merc crackles into the gravel and settles into a place.

"it just needs gas... i ran out of gas."
"i'll tell palko to bring some on the truck."

the sheriff is back on the radio, the little man is closing the doors of the hearse with his own quiet ceremony, i'm sitting in the merc with the door open, my left leg hanging out, watching the rain dot the road.

"all right boys, i've got a call back at the lake, you hang tight, palko will be here with the tow truck in twenty minutes or so, and stay off the road, we don't need anyone getting killed ... sorry about your loss, son."
"thank you."

the cruiser backs up, turns around and drives away with
the purpose of speed. it's like he was never here. the ravens
are gone. the rain is spaced out like the first parts of a rain
does, it feels good on my arms and salt. the little man is
in the driver's seat of the hearse, the window is down, but
he's leaning into the middle of the car so his jacket won't
get wet. i walk up to the window where it all started and
let the rain confess for me, waiting to say anything until
i feel soaked.

"thank you, i'll pay for all the damage and the tow truck."
"yes, you will."
"i'm sorry. i'm sorry i said you were just a delivery service."
"and a bad barber."
"i didn't mean to diminish what you do, i'm just a little off
balance, it's been a rough couple of days."
"it's understandable, it's my duty to try to help the deceased
and their survivors thru the process. the good thing is you
won't remember much."
"jesus, i don't think i'll ever forget this."
"you'll remember a version of what happened, you won't
remember 'this', i've seen worse."
"worse than this, jesus christ, i ran you off the road."
"oh yes, well this might be the worse, but no one was hurt.
people do things not normally in their character when
they're under stress, i've had poor souls throw themselves

into graves after their loved ones, fist fights over jewelry, pulling rings and such right off the body."

"oh god, all right maybe i don't feel so bad, anyway thanks for handling everything with that sheriff."

"you're welcome."

"god, i'm having a fucked up day ...a fucking week."

"sometimes we just have to let go and let god."

"oh jesus..."

"exactly."

"i was raised catholic, but i don't believe in any of it anymore."

"well, we often wind up where we started, you might be surprised what you fall back on in times like these."

"yeah ... i guess."

"do you want to accompany the body."

"to the crematorium?"

"yes, often times the next of kin accompany the body."

"no, i think i'm done."

"we'll have the ashes at the mortuary for you by monday, with the holy weekend it's going to take a couple of days, your mother is aware of the arrangements."

"yeah, thank you, i'll leave my insurance information at your office, is that okay?"

"yes, that will be fine."

"thanks again ... take care of him."

"i will."

take care of him? i don't know what else to say. i turn away and walk up the road to the mercury, trying to walk between the rain and the ripening storm, feeling like i might disappear. i wonder if the little man is watching me, i don't know what else will keep me here. i'm alone in my head, inside my terrible ideas, alone on this road and the world now. my past is mine and hers and i hate her. the car smells of him and my wet hair. everything is only the rain, the only sound, everything i see melting down the windows and into the ground. i've finally vanished, i'm almost free, maybe dead and relieved of anything, but this water.

"hey. hey! wake up, i got your gas, you owe me eight bucks and another fifty for the tow, kapelka said you're paying."

there's a shadow inside a yellow slicker yelling in thru the glass above the rain. the sky has fallen.

"what?"

i roll the window down.

"you owe me fifty eight bucks for the tow and the gas."

i raise my hips forward and dig into my pocket, the rain is pouring into the open window.

"all i have is twenties, here's sixty."
"i ain't got change, so it's sixty then."
"that's fine."
"hell, i shoulda said sixty one."
"yeah, i guess."

the yellow dream dissolves into the tow truck and the deluge, what it seems we brought on somehow. the hearse drives by slowly, the little man looking over at me like he doesn't see me and i wonder if i'm here. i'm afraid to look, even for my hands on the wheel. i watch the hearse's taillights move down the road instead, into a colorless rain and across the center line of my life. everything from now on will be always after and before and marked by high waters on a perishing memory and the exposed roots of the trees and the near bridge.

6

they say the year i was born was a particularly wet year, the old men who knew about such things, the month i was born a water sign, what the old women said. i don't remember what i looked like, but i remember what the world looked like, the rife of trees and the elephant sky and always water, always the threat of rain and the life of the river and the end of everything at the beginning of the lake. it is the same water, what washes down on me now, what once ran under ground, under my grape skin, cutting the ravine in front of the old house, the same way wove into the cloth bones that braid my back. i am only water and calcium it seems, bits of iron and salts, everything starting in our mother's waters and a god's right whisper wet in our ears. the rain is made of the great lake, the river is made of three creeks and riddles of rain. it runs winding thru the woods and thru a kindness of soft sandstone, around the long-suffering granite that plagues it's path. indians ran here too i'm told, but they don't run here anymore. where they got to i'll never know, another bit of chaos and finality that my father could never quite explain, nor would he try unless he knew twenty seven chippewa or was reading from the sunday plain dealer out loud.

my parents reached a certain age and i held them there, always forty, maybe forty five, in my mind. my mother's red hair and her moon face, my father with his barn sided hands and his teeth in his mouth, the scent of his work skin like the memory of an animal. their faces folded and see thru now, all my toy ideas of them wrecked with this jealous time and what a life does. all i can see is the sight of her in her bed, bent and covered with dew and dod-dering around cracked and dry by afternoon, the old man dead and blue and just ashes sometime today and never anything more. i can't think about his soul, but i wonder where his smoke will go.

i wonder if i've changed, my face turning into a story i don't know, driving the old man's car like i drove some twenty years ago and the river road and looking at myself in the side view mirror and the pearls of rain around me. the windshield wipers rub back and forth as futile as any mark of time and space, counting out the clicks until it's clear, until everything disappears into the ground and the miles until the gravel again and the house ahead in the rain like always.

she's standing on the back porch like she never left, i pull the merc up, turn the key back, put its whittled engine to rest. i leave the keys in the ignition, he left the keys in the ignition, he'd say "if they want it they can have it" and close the door. i close the door. i'm soaked thru my clothes, i'm not even wet i'm only part of the rain. she's in the kitchen when i walk in, standing next to the cluttered kitchen table like some proud fisherman posing for the local paper with a twelve pound pike. there's newspapers and books and an old radio playing even older music and plastic containers and pans with aluminum foil and cans of food with their labels peeled away long ago.

"ellen brought over a pork roast and a green bean casserole to put in the oven, she's such a love."
"who's ellen?"
"oh you know, ellen and the kids."
"i don't remember them."
"you remember art and ellen, and i sent you pictures of david and lizzy, i say lizzy, ellen insists on elizabeth, but she hates it."
"i haven't lived here for twenty years or something, mom, i don't know who art and ellen are and i don't remember

getting pictures of their children, i'm sorry."

"it's okay dear, maybe they moved here after you'd gone."

"i'm soaked and i'm starving, do we have anything i can eat now?"

"it's been raining like this for weeks, do you want some jello? judy brought a beautiful jello mold over. why didn't you eat in town?"

"you didn't call kapelka's did you?"

"i did."

"i had to chase him down the river road, why didn't he wait?"

"mary karen said john had already left."

"then don't ask me why i didn't eat breakfast in town, what am i going to do, never see dad again. i had to see him on the side of the road, in the back of the god damn hearse!"

"you should change out of those wet clothes before you get chilled."

"i almost didn't see dad, it's been twelve years!"

"you're father's at peace now, james, what you saw isn't your father, your father's gone on to god."

"well it's all i've got, that was the last time i'll ever see him."

"nicole called here while you were out."

i feel my chest pour into the ground like the rain pouring down the gutter downspout along the porch and into a rusted culvert in the front yard. i push my tongue into my teeth like i do, before i can say anything, until i taste blood.

"did you talk with her?"

"the phone has been ringing constantly since your father died, i had twenty three phone messages yesterday."

"mom, what did nikki say?"

"she wished me well, she said she was sorry she couldn't be here."

"did she say anything else?"

"nicole asked me not to tell you that she called, i don't want to get in the middle of you two."

"i'm your son!"

"i'm finally at peace with your father gone, i can meditate and pray and do my exercises, i don't want any more drama. i'm staying out of yours and nicole's business."

"thanks a lot."

"my mother was always looking over my shoulder, sticking her nose in, she loved your father though."

"i could use some support right now."

"i'm not going to pick sides."

i can only walk away from her and the consumption of her talk, out of the web of the kitchen, into the hall, my throat like a clenched hand.

"god, i hate you."

i say it so she can't hear me, i've always said it so she couldn't hear. it's not even a word, hate, as much as a shadow on my lung, the moment after a breath and before another, a doubt. something i bring inside of me and hold and let out, but never all of it out. some part of it i keep, somehow i need it, my life fueled on it, burning like an oil fire in a noon-day sun and black, it's soot everywhere i walk and seemingly endless. i'm at my end, anger is all i have left. it's familiar and safe, something to swirl around in my mouth before i swallow good. i'm at the bottom of the steps. i can hear her church voice, she's talking on the phone.

"i told judy ... the memorial's monday at saint joseph's ... i'm fine, i couldn't be better, he's finally at peace, i'm at peace, thank god ... james is here from california ... oh yes, father ciolek, he loved ben ... well they're both czech ..."

i can hear the rattle of her head and her toothy smile, something a dull child might draw on the wall and finally just my feet on the stairs, the bed springs of my old bed, my old escape act as if i were fifteen, the clemency of the rain on the roof so there's no other sound. there's scotch tape still on my bedroom door where i hung a poster of pete townshend bearded like a jesus on a three day bender. his anger burned down to sadness, the oil fires burning black into the backs of my eyes still.

7

my father never learned to swim or even how to drown, he died in his sleep in his bed. and yet he spent his days in the river or on the lake, in a fed-up aluminum boat or along the muddy sides or in the shallows up to his waist. i wonder if the water filled his dreams like it still fills mine, but i can only wonder and wade into my sleep and feel for the bottom with my good foot. my father collected biological samples for the city college and the university and the state and federal water regulatory agencies. he wasn't a biologist, but a chemist, the world wrote out with the periodic chart, that's what he'd say and all he saw i suppose. he was a simple man despite the theorems and equations he was burdened with, the son of a working man, his father a farmer on this cleared land, a factory worker and a drunk.

my father was an alcoholic, my mother a sort of side stage vaudeville act, but i only know that now, it was all i knew then. every night the crease of her in her green camaro down the gravel road, the hum of him wrapped in the dark and darker in his angry chair. every night him drinking to himself, a single ice cube and a thick finger of gallon bourbon in a greasy gas station glass, what he got for free with a fill up and a dollar off coupon for the car wash he'd never use. every night his insides curving outward into time, his hair receding back, his mind whirring like the high tension wires that run thru the woods to the city from the electric plant up the lake. his eyes seemed bottomless looking into his glass and secret like the deep waters where the teeth pike schooled, the television flicker on his face, at first black and white and later on, color. and it would fall late and come time for bed and he would be screaming 'fuck this' and 'fuck that' at the t.v., at my mother when she was home or at the space she left when she went down the gravel road, something only he could see. and he would look down at me with a strangely forgiving face and say everything without saying a word. and me with my soda pop eyes looking up and never forgiving myself for some sin that seemed to make him so sad.

i'm walking downstairs into the cellar, what was his cellar, into the root truth of this house and all that's left of him.

a single light bulb above the brittle steps, the yellow smell of time and black mildew, the brown trap of his disease the light can't push away. there's salt between the stone blocks where the rain leaches in and wet now. i can hear her above me in the awful ceiling, on the floor boards like a mouse chewing at its teeth. she's playing "her irish music", what she calls it like it's no one else's. i turn the switch at the end of the cellar stairs like i might know him, a fluorescent utility light buzzes and troubles my father's work shop and almost the corners, but not behind the furnace or the water heater where my young nightmares bred, where all the dark shines from and the ghosts of all the spiders i've killed crowd and crouch down and wait. he never killed them, he always carried them outside.

my father kept everything, everything in sample glass bottles with black plastic lids and a place for a label, everything in coffee cans and cardboard boxes and borrowed milk crates, everything in stacks and piles and strewn everywhere in the end. screen doors and screwdrivers and old carpets and wire, wire fences and boards and scrap pieces of wood, broken saws, one rusted but still with all its teeth and wrenches and pliers, old paint brushes petrified, buckets of paint surely dried and forgotten and stacked to hold a plank to make a shelf to hold more cans of varnish and linoleum glue. there were cans of food too and two broken televisions, old radios and clocks and a chain saw and lengths of nylon rope and a rusted anchor. everything virtually random and senseless like a galaxy spinning around some dark matter i couldn't conceive, maybe a pennsylvania road map or a toy train at the center, playboy magazines, '67's and '71's and nothing in between, everything he ever owned or anything that crossed his path twisting into his darkness, into the gravity of his past he couldn't use or throw away.

"your father always said we should just burn the house down when he's dead and start over."

her voice from the top of the stairs like a weak conscience, she won't come down. she never came down.

"it's an idea."

my voice up thru the floor boards from the gut of the house more like a feeling than a thought.

"look through everything and put aside what you want, the boys are coming tomorrow to start throwing things out, i'm getting one of those dumpsters, they can pull it right up into the driveway."
"mom, maybe you could give me a couple of days, there's a lot here, it's a lot to try to deal with."
"i want to get started, will you do me one favor and take

your father's chair from the living room outside."

"now?"

"i want it out of this house, it's broken, he insisted on keeping that damn chair, it's ridiculous."

"when i'm done down here i'll do it, it's pouring outside right now."

"frank stuckley is coming this afternoon if it stops raining to take a look at the porch and the roof where the raccoons have tore a hole, they're living in the attic."

"mom, why don't you just take it easy a little bit, i mean dad's only been dead for like thirty hours or something."

"i've lived with your father's illness for forty two years and i'm not living in it anymore, not another day, i won't."

"these are dad's things i don't want some strangers picking thru all his stuff, even if it is all a pile of shit, it's his pile of shit."

"your father loved the boys, he'd make soup for me to take over to theresa's every saturday."

"i don't want anyone to see this."

"the boys know what went on."

"what are you talking about?"

"theresa and the boys."

"who's theresa and the boys?"

"you know, brett and chuck."

"i don't know."

"well maybe if you would have been more a part of our

lives... but i know you love california, i'd never tell you to come back home."

"come back to what? look at this place, it's an insane asylum."

"letting go was the hardest thing i've ever done, you're my only child."

"i don't think you let me go, i think i ran for my life."

"if that's what you think maybe you should just go back to california now, you won't ever have to deal with me again."

"i'm not saying that."

"i'm fine, my friends all say 'how can your only child live so far away' but i'm fine, i know you're happy there."

"mom, i had to get out of this house. if anyone can understand that it should be you."

"i had to learn to accept the things i couldn't change, james. it's hard, but with god's graces anything is possible."

the cellar will stay something she's never seen, the brown and bile of him, her husband's life in one big pile, what he made of his sickness like a suspicious dark spot on a chest x-ray. this is her house and the dogma she lives by, the denial that keeps her faith alive and holds up the roof. every word she says becomes only prayers, rosary beads and repetitions, catchy phrases from alanon.

there are shouts and secrets in boxes and strewn on the

floor. under a ravaged box of frosted flakes is the timex i remember him wearing, in a shoebox of four other frightened watches i don't remember and broken bands, a lifetime of watches, an elgin engraved, 'to my darling, ben, '60'. her voice from up the stairs again like she's come down from the mountain.

"james, i'm leaving for saint joseph's, i'm chanting the noon mass, we won't be done until three when jesus is finally dead."

"what?"

"i have to sing tonight and all day tomorrow for holy saturday and of course we have three masses for easter sunday, leave it to your father to die during holy week."

"we're going to have to talk about dad's funeral."

"we will... loretta is picking me up so you don't have to worry about me driving in this rain."

"the gravel road is really wet."

"it rains about this time every good friday."

"where do you come up with this stuff? it rains all spring, mom."

"it's all recorded in the bible."

"whatever."

"are you finding everything you want?"

"i don't know."

"your father wanted you to have everything, he always said 'you and james are the only people i love, god rest his soul."

"there's a lifetime down here, mom, i don't even know where to start, hell my toys are probably where i left them thirty years ago."

"your father didn't throw anything out, that was his way, it was his space, i left him alone down there."

"where did this all come from?"

"he saved everything, james. there's things left from the old farm house after the big flood. every week he'd come home with the craziest things he found in the river or the lake."

"yeah, i just don't know what to do with a cream separator in my apartment."

"i haven't been down there in years."

"i didn't think you ever came down here."

"once, when your father and i were first married, oh, i think that's loretta, help yourself to the pork, dear ... bye bye ... there's jello!"

i can hear the timing of a car engine, a woman named loretta and a car door shut, all of it squeezed thru the tiny window up near the ceiling of the cellar and just above the ground. the rain has made the glass muddy so everything is only an impression, some part of the rain and the earth. i'm alone in the house now, i feel like an armless ghost banging around downstairs. i'm here with him now, surrounded by his sickness, the sticks he stacked up to make a life. i don't trust myself by myself or the shirt stain of him i'm wearing. i'm afraid he's too much a part

of me for me to ever be anything else. i was always afraid
of the cellar and the dark beneath the steps and behind
the furnace and the water heater. i'm afraid of myself now
and the dark inside me, something i caught from him like
a cough i can't pay for, something there when i open up
my mouth in the mirror.

8

"nik, it's me."

we had one telephone and one television, a console t.v. in front of my father's brown chair. the phone was in the kitchen among the kitchen things and somehow alone like the victim of a rape, every conversation ever at the end of a three foot cord and never further. i could only talk for so long, any longer was "just crap" and i was told to hang up, the old man yelling whenever the phone rang and threatening to tear it out of the wall. it was a black rotary phone then, a bulky beige push button phone from the seventies now, probably something he found, and a shaky voiced answering machine next to it from the radio shack in town, black plastic and a simulated wood grain. he kept his liquor in the cabinet beneath it like a bad joke. the door around the handle blackened from his hands, from the river and the years. and i suddenly thought of his gut and the black there, a dark that tore at his heart and finally broke loose two nights ago and broke him for good. something you could never see, but see coming. something you could only feel around him and wonder where it sprung from and never know.

i was a wire then, a brick wall now and something to see and sinews and smiles that were finally just grins. i was something between the rain, i was seventeen and almost invisible. i could coil down the stairs like the soundless ghosts of deer that ate at my mother's rhododendron and call my girlfriend, mary ann amari, every middle of the night when the house was mine. i'd sit and listen to the house breathe in and out the dark, the old man snoring thru his pricker patch sleep, drank black and ruined by birds. and her in between him and the fan blades, a noth-ingness below the sounds of another night. it would be too hot to sleep. it was that summer and she was fifteen and it all made sense. i'd open his cabinet under the counter while we talked and marvel at the amber of bushmills and jim beam and the cheap bourbon he drank every day, bottles of rum and vodka, drambuie and gin. i stared at them like diamonds when the moon was right and sniffed at and sipped a bit of their spell like a loose dog might or a witch. and i sat on the floor and we talked into the night until it was almost light, about what i won't remember. i somehow remember her skin though, or the thought of her skin and the smell of breck shampoo and that we were about to grow up. i remember it was the first time i felt happy, but i was young then and i lived my life like i had a chance and a chance to forget.

"james?"
"yeah."
"are you okay?"
"yeah, i'm okay. it was a long trip, though. we flew straight into a goddamn thunder storm, i thought we were going to go right into the lake."
"is it strange to be home?"
"god, the house is a disaster, i don't even know how to describe it. the ceiling is falling in, there's raccoons in the attic, i could hear them when it wasn't raining, it's been raining constantly except for when i first got here, the old man has buckets everywhere and piles of shit up over the windows, it's like living inside his fucked up head."
"i don't know what to..."
"ah shit..."

there is a flicker, a gasp of light, then nothing. i wonder if his heart went the same. if he laid speechless, trapped in the last moments of his mind til the red blood it had left turned to blue and finally black. everywhere is only the color of the storm, but down the hall where her candles are burning yellow in her bedroom. some things seem more in the dark, the rain louder, the lengths of my breaths, the shadows from her saints burning next to the television, but most things seem small next to the storm and it's gray. i am small, my voice stretched into a wire and black on the other end.

"nik?"

"i'm here, what's wrong?"

"now the electricity's gone out, it must be the storm, i guess the phone lines are okay."

"can you stay in a hotel."

"there's a motel in town, but it's like twenty minutes, half hour in this shit, they'll get it going again, it's a regular thing out here. anyway i've got so much to do at the house i can't leave."

"it's still daylight there isn't it?"

"this house is always dark with the woods, and with this storm... it doesn't matter, she's got candles burning everywhere."

"what are you going to do?"

"i don't even know where to start, my mother actually made up their bed for us... for me, to sleep in, the bed my old man just died in yesterday, she's totally nuts."

"how's your mother doing?"

"she's fine i guess, i don't know, she's completely insane, she's off singing at church all weekend, it's holy week."

"well maybe that will keep her mind off of things for a while."

"her husband just died. i think she needs to deal with a few things."

"i just meant it might make things easier for her."

"she's organizing my father's memorial service like it's some sort of anniversary party or something."

"well they were together a pretty long time, she probably hasn't accepted your father's death yet."

" 'oh he's at peace now'! that's all she can fucking say, 'your father's at peace, now.' she's almost ecstatic, she's so wrapped up in all her catholic bullshit she'll never see anything even close to reality."

"maybe that's the best place for her."

"maybe, maybe that's all i'll ever have, a father who drank himself to death and some crazy mother making up my father's death bed. nik, there's bottles everywhere and piles of old shit and garbage and her fucking candles lit everywhere and this god damn irish music blaring from her room."

"you're just going to be there a couple of days."

"i'm drowning in it, i don't know what i'm going to do... nik, i need you."

"you'll survive, you always do."

"what's that supposed to mean?"

"i have to go."

her voice breaks on the word 'go', the kind of silence that is the sound of crying. i feel a lifetime sink into my side, the river spill into the lake, and in that bead of time i finally realize how i've hurt her, how i hurt myself. her crying somewhere in san francisco in some apartment i don't know, my own tears from somewhere deep, somewhere so deep it's behind me and only part of me.

"i miss you."
"i know."
"that's all you can say, i know? i feel like i've lost both my arms."
"i can't talk anymore, it's all too much still, i've got to go, take care of yourself."
"nik ..... nik?

there's a click and the sound of no sound in the receiver, something like an empty closet, a cattle of rain outside, the lonesome smell of the house, the dust all around me, pieces probably of their skin and their old fingernails, maybe even mine from years ago.

"... i love you."

i hang up the phone and pick it back up and start to call her ... one, four, one, five... before i hang up again. i lean against the wall and let my back slide down the rotten paint where he brushed against until it was his. i'm sitting on the floor, i'm forty, i'm living out a circle, something i drew in the sand and maybe a spiral down.

i take a candle from the credenza and open the cabinet
and look in like i might be reading someone's diary. i feel
compelled to look behind me, but i know i'm alone. i turn
around and look anyway. it's in there still, a family's history,
my livered legacy, some almost empty, their labels curled at
the corners, some nearly full, handled and half galloned,
cheap grocery store brands in clear plastic bottles, bottles
of vodka and a canadian whiskey bottled in new jersey.
they're silent and left unspoken, one is talked down and
feels like a murder, probably what he drank before he went
to bed his last night. there's a quantity of desperation, no
romantic notion, no bottle of jack and a glass, but cheap
booze in the cabinet and two liter bottles of seven-up and a
blue cup that says saint joseph's summer bizarre in yellow
sitting on the kitchen table, the practical sustenance of this
sickness and everyday plastic.

"james what are you doing? dear."
"what are you doing back?"

i close the cabinet door, guilty of something if only telling
a secret to myself out loud.

"loretta dropped me off just before the bridge, with the
river and all this rain, she was afraid to drive down the
gravel road again, she almost didn't get out the first time,
it's been raining for weeks, it's mostly just mud now."

"but why aren't you at mass?"

"the river road's flooded we couldn't get to saint joseph's or mass. we drove all the way to the wood bridge before we had to turn around."

"mom, what happened here?"

"oh, the lights have been going on and off for weeks, it's been raining like i've never seen it, not since you were born at least."

"i don't mean the power, i mean... never mind."

she can only go to her room, to the call of her candles, to the small altar she has there, a picture and a daffodil. i can only stare into the cabinet with what little light there is left from the storm, from a candle in the hall. this is the last bits of him, what didn't kill him unlike all the bottles before, pieces of rain that never made it to the river, our broken hopes that we could ever be anything else.

9

she's in her room, what was the spare bed-
room downstairs. his chair is in the living room there, a
childhood fear i forgot and live with and wear just beneath
my smile. it's a different chair than the burden i grew up
with, but the same chair, always his chair, always hack-
neyed upholstery, something plaid and filthy from him and
his bohunk skin, sitting with his shirt off in the summer,
surely, and a ring of the river, something i can almost
hear. it's filled with the dark like he's still there, sloping
to the left where its front leg has broken off, its posture is
disturbing like the bent walk of a killer, almost menacing
like a stranger noticing your shoes. it's more a part of him
than the waxen rind of him in kapelka's hearse. this is the
juice of him, spit and vomit, acid and bile, this chair where
he raged and wrung his hands like he did, like he might
squeeze the blood out of them, his father's blood and his,

a blood he could only thin with alcohol and never cure. i can feel his anger, a stain of sadness now, something in me like a vein of coal deep in the ground, something black and ready to burn, his memory my memory, nights in the t.v. light and a curled up t.v. guide from the sunday paper, whiskey in the winter, beer in the summer, sitting in the dark, and him even darker against the night.

"oh thank god! you're throwing that horrible chair out."
"yeah, i guess ...
"ughh, that chair broke years ago, but your father, well you know the way he was, throwing it out and getting a new chair, he wouldn't hear of it."
"mom, this is beyond just being cheap, this is crazy, the chair, the cellar, lights that don't work, the sinks, christ, the whole house is falling apart, people don't live like this."
"your father was a sick man."
"you live here too."
"there's nothing i could've done, james, your father was an alcoholic, i had to accept that."
"you didn't have to live like this."
"i loved your father very much, for better or for worse, he was a good man."
"he was a son of a bitch."
"don't you dare say that!"
"i think i earned that right."

"he loved you, he always talked about you. the poor man had a disease, james."

"he was a fucking drunk."

"he tried, james."

"i don't have a single memory of him without a glass in his hand, him screaming and yelling every night."

"he never would of hurt you."

"well he did."

"your father never laid a hand on you."

"i was scared shitless of him."

"it was the alcohol, james, it wasn't your father."

"the end result's the same."

"you turned out fine, look at everything you've accomplished in california."

"i haven't turned out fine."

"you're a very successful artist, that man at the gallery, mr. lewis says you're a real talent."

"his name is lowe and he hasn't sold a fucking piece of mine. i'm a welder for caltrans, mom, and that's it, nothing more."

"you're a good man, james."

"bullshit, i'm fucked up."

"you've done so much."

"the only thing i've done is break every heart i've known, including my own."

"relationships are a two way street."

"god you and these cliches, you've got an answer for everything."

"the answer is prayer."

"yeah, just look around, look at what all your prayers did for you, wow."

"i pray for strength, james, strength and acceptance."

"acceptance? when are you going to accept that the old man treated us like shit."

"you wouldn't exist if it wasn't for your father."

"that's such bullshit."

"it's true."

"whatever, i don't owe either one of you."

"your father did a lot for you."

"yeah like drinking himself into oblivion every night."

"your father and i were married for forty-two years."

"so what?"

"so i know your father pretty darn well. when he was sober he was a kind, giving man."

"fuck him! he was a drunk and a fucking coward."

"yes, your father drank himself to death."

"oh wow, there's some news."

"you think you know what happened here? let me tell you what happened here while you were living your 'poor miserable' life in california. your father reached the point where he was drinking all day, first thing in the morning till he finally passed out in the evening. the smell from those damn bottles, he burned the plastic bottles in the fireplace because he was embarrassed to throw them out, he was drinking a bottle a day if not more. he didn't shower, but once a week, he didn't change his clothes, he didn't have a tooth left in his mouth at the end, he wouldn't go to the dentist or the doctor. i saw him grabbing his chest coming back from the river that wednesday afternoon, i asked him what he wanted to do and he told me he just wanted to die, that's all he wanted, so i let him."

"was he in pain?"

"your father died in his sleep that night like i told you. he ran his finger down my back like he did sometimes if we'd been fighting just to say he was sorry and that was it, i knew he was gone, i could feel the life pass right out of him ... my darling ben."

it's the first time i've seen her cry since i've been home, small faithful tears, quiet as her bookshelf madonna or any, the weight of her catholic gracefully upon her, crushing her, the resignation of sadness suckling at her breast. i'm embarrassed to watch her, unable to really feel for her or comfort her, but i watch her like i might never see her again, running my memory over her tears like her worn fingers over her rosary beads. it's the first time i've ever seen her eyes and i realize that if i ever loved her i only feel sorry for her now.

"why didn't you tell me what was going on?"

"your father didn't want you to see him like he was, he looked terrible. you have your life in california, i knew when you left you'd never come back, i didn't want you to come back, not to this, i knew you were happy."

"how did it get like this? it was always bad, but this is... incredible."

"your father would be out at the river all morning, i'm not sure how he could even do his work anymore, he was drinking first thing, i'll never get it out of my head how his hands would shake when he'd get up out of bed in the morning. he'd bring home his samples and he'd be down in his workshop doing whatever he did down there, i didn't have the schooling to understand his work, your father was a brilliant man. i'm sure he was drinking all day. by evening he could hardly function, he'd sleep in his chair until sometime in the night when he'd finally come up to bed, he'd reek of the booze and the river."

"and i suppose you were at church day and night praying for him."

"i watched your father die every day, james, he was beyond anything i could do, some things you have to leave up to god."

"that's convenient."

"your father had no choice, he had to drink."

"i don't buy into all your alanon shit, of course he had a choice."

"he didn't! alcoholism is a disease."

"bullshit, cancer is a disease, alcohol is a conscious choice, he chose to drink, he chose to live in this hell, you chose to live with him. i'm the one that didn't have any choices, not until i was eighteen at least and i could get the fuck out of here."

"all this profanity... you sound just like him."

i pick up the chair like some dime store hercules, my face pressed against it, all of him pressed against me, how many years of his earth and sweat. i carry it down the hall and thru the kitchen, the screen door tearing, the door's aluminum latch breaking, my arms rip thru the door frame. i throw it to the ground from the porch, all of it and him and their history hit the river rock and splinter and hold together by the upholstery like a stubborn body of broken bones. goddamn him. goddamn her.

i stare down at this effigy of our sorrow and suddenly remember it's good friday. i wonder what they did with christ's body after they took him down and what they did with his cross. i look back at the wall jesus she has hanging in the kitchen. a rock star looking savior looking down on me and perfectly and sad still and a stabbing thought of nikki's face closed tight with tears and the memory of my father's blue face looking up like he might be relieved. i'm bleeding red into the rain, blue veins running down my arm. i can feel her behind me in the kitchen like some nagging thought i'll soon forget, but be bothered trying to remember. she won't say a word, it's like none of it ever happened, any of it, ever. goddamn me.

10

it was a warm rain, something from the south and our imaginations, something between this world and the next and larger than us, the rain small pieces of everything we'd lost and tried to forget. i stood on the back porch for what would seem like hours maybe to a dead man, a minute to a man that's just dying. i was surviving if not living, my arm torn open, but nothing, my blood mixing with the water, with the mud and back to where i started, i guess. i lived here eighteen years before i left. i've lived here my whole life somehow.

we only talked of the weather, of the buckeyes and the browns, the old man and me. he would have known it rained the last nineteen days out of twenty, how many inches of rain we had and how many feet the river rose. the river was as high as any time i remember, its waters certain and secret and somehow bigger than the earth. only the great will of the lake kept it to its destiny, but not before it broke its banks and made its way into the trees and up their trunks and over the road into the hollows.

"i'm on the phone with janice stuckley, frank can't make it, she's saying the river's flooding even up as far as the highway and parts of the river road, no one can get in or out of town except for tim burgermeister with that ridiculous truck of his."

"great, i guess i'm eating pork and jello for the weekend."

"father had to cancel good friday and he's cancelled holy saturday and probably easter mass."

"does god know father's canceling the resurrection of his son?"

"james, don't be a smart aleck ... oh it's just james being silly ... janice says we're the ones that don't know, faith is about belief, god's work is always a mystery ... oh he just laughing at us ... well i'm going to meditate and sing regardless... janice, i've been rehearsing for weeks and i'm singing, i don't care if it's at saint joseph's or here at home, the show must go on ..."

i can hear her thru the house as i walk upstairs, her phone conversation like a bug in the wall. i find a yellowed box of band aids in the medicine cabinet, in the only bathroom in the house, upstairs next to their bedroom. the white

metal cabinet no different than before, but plastic disposable razors now instead of the old safety blades, crest
toothpaste crudded at the end, frayed toothbrushes, bayer
aspirin and an unused box of dental floss, probably the
same reel i never used. i step into their room like i'm stepping into cold water. i put my father's slicker on gingerly
like i'm sinking into the river. i stiffen, it smells of him, a
memory of him around its greasy collar, stained cuffs and
arm pits, my memory and my childhood, the river and his
day beard, bourbon whiskey and the mennon aftershave
he got from her every christmas, the box always wrapped
in green, the label always saying, 'to ben from james', as
if she couldn't bear to give him anything.

i walk down the stairs and past her in the kitchen on the
phone still. my feet in his rubber boots as if i ever wore
my own shoes. i wince at the thought and with each step,
his steps maybe. i open the broken screen door, it doesn't
close, it's only hanging from its bottom hinge, the screen
torn, its frame bent and buckled like aluminum does, his
chair below heartbroken on the river rock and the gravel
in the rain. i pull it into the air and carry it to the shed
house, i feel myself crying, he's dead now, i know it. i didn't
know it until now. i can hear the unconscious of the river,
even above the rain and the rain on the slicker's hood that
i have loosely over my head and the sound of my snot and
my feet on the gravel and his boots.

the shed smells like i imagine an old man would smell, the dense smell of a long life collected, things you used you can't use anymore, things you lost that you still have and just can't find. there's a light coming in the cracks between the flat boards, something gray and all the storm will allow. the roof is leaking, the doors are stubborn, their metal rollers whine with rust and hate as i push them apart with effort to their sides. my sled is still hanging on a six penny nail, my old bike, flat tired and forlorn behind the garbage cans. i always wanted a purple schwinn, i got my cousin's old orange bike from sears instead, the disappointment of ten and kept in the shed. i hadn't thought of it in years and there it is in the corner and in the spider webs strung across it's handle bars and thru my chest. there's shovels, flat shovels and round, a broken handle and a snow shovel and axes and a spud bar, a crow bar and another pry tool, a maddox and a pick, if there's a difference, and several sledge hammers like he forget he had one, rusted wedges and attentive fishing poles between the wall studs and a net and his tackle box filled with a mystery of lures and my old tackle box left open and confused with nails now and screws and washers and estranged bolts. i push his old chair to a corner next to an old console television i don't remember. oil stains on the cement floor from his old truck or the comet or the mercury. everything here we choose to forget, but keep because we somehow have to, because it is what we are.

"what are you doing?"

she's yelling from the porch door still in the kitchen.

"i'm putting dad's chair out of the way for now till you get the dumpster!"

i'm lying, i can't bear to see it or to throw it away, some way to forget what i'll always remember.

"do you want to hear the hymns we rehearsed for church? i thought i'd sing them for you!"
"no, i'm going to walk the gravel road, take a look at what's going on with the river before it gets too dark!"
"you're just like your father, the two of you and that river!"
"i'm not anything like him and i don't want to be."
"your father was a beautiful man when he was sober, he had a lot of wonderful qualities."
"yeah, and exactly when was that?"
"your father took care of you when you were first born, i had rheumatic fever and i couldn't be near you, i was sick for months. he'd hold you up at the door so i could see you. you'd be curled up in his hands. you have your father's hands, james and your father's eyes... he'd carry you down to the river in an old back pack with your bottles and diapers so he could work."

i've come out of the garage into the rain like i just saw
the world for the first time. so much of me that i never
knew.

"i guess that was the only time he was sober."
"he had his moments, he quit for seven months when i
moved out."
"you moved out of the house?"
"we thought it was best not to tell you."
"how could you not tell me?
"we didn't want you to be upset."
"where did you stay?"
"in the city, i had a beautiful apartment looking over the
lake, your father was so sweet, he'd shower and shave and
drive into the city every sunday and meet me after mass,
saint ignatius is a beautiful cathedral. we'd have lunch
and he'd drive home. he'd be sober the whole afternoon,
it was like we were dating."
"i don't know why you moved back."
"oh, your father missed me, and my life is here, i have
my friends and alanon and saint josephs. everything was
wonderful, your father wasn't drinking, he'd lost all that
puffiness in his face, you know it was the booze, and then
we went to your damn uncle's for christmas and that was
it, i'll never forgive martin for that, he brought ben a drink
and that was the end of it."

"mom, he never quit, i don't believe that. he probably hid it from you and drank a little less, but i can't believe he quit."

"he did quit, i know it, god gave me that gift of a few months."

"so was god punishing you the rest of the time?"

"james, such talk, god's mercy is endless, i have so many blessings, most of all i have the blessing of faith."

"why didn't you move out again after uncle martin's ?"

"i'm tired."

"why wouldn't you leave when he started to drink again?"

"i'm going to lay down for a while, i'm exhausted."

"jesus christ, why can't you answer me?"

"i told you i'm tired, james. i'm going to take a nap and get up and finish the plans for your father's memorial on monday."

"forget it."

"james, i need to ask one favor of you, will you go through your father's liquor cabinet and the rest of the house and collect all the bottles together, raymond gave me a list of what he needs for the reception, i hope we'll have enough."

"who's raymond?"

"he bartends for the saint joseph's reception hall."

"i thought the memorial is going to be in the morning."

"ten o'clock, holy monday."

"does it strike you as a bit ironic that you're going to fully stock a bar for dad's memorial at ten in the morning when he just drank himself to death?"

"i'm just doing what raymond asked for."

"you're an idiot!"

i can hear my father out of me like puke, i want to spit or tell her i'm sorry. she's already walked away singing some song through the kitchen, trading lies with her god. i walk up the gravel road with the rain and his smell around me instead. i'm lost in our memory and our blood, in the storm livid sky and everything brooding into night. the sky has gone black like a toenail, the trees just black ideas and a space where the gravel road runs, a feeling more than something i can see. i can hear the river, maybe her sobbing. i can hear his bawl and my halloo, the broken women around us, something ringing in my head, another ghost, headlights moving through the trees like news, like towny bar talk of a small town tragedy.

it's the start of a story, a hard rain, a rain you will remember always. a storm the townies will speak of years later in slim voices saved for last loves or rumors of summer cabin murders. it is something whispered at grocery store checkout lines amongst polyester fettered women or the grim talk of the men smoking short cigarettes down by the lake. it is only and everything like your god, like the idea

of a stranger moving thru the trees, a light on the curve of
the gravel road. it is the animal center of my spine, a fear
rising up in me like the rising river over its banks, over my
head. everything is soundless and only part of the storm
so there's nothing else, but the slur of my thoughts. i'm
in my secret now, inside this rain and the shoebox where
i keep my soft middle.

i'm gathered into a shadow, a hand made into a fist. i've
made myself into a rock, but rocks brittle and break. i
want to turn myself into water, something yielding and
ultimately unbending, something that's always known and
knows where it's going, something that can remember
without thinking, without judgment or the prejudice of
stone. and i'll bleed into the earth, become part of the
whole again, and never pray again or bear the burden of
these thoughts.

i'm walking to the start of everything, to the end of us,
to the river and all our roots. our histories stuck in the
river's side like the river is stuck in our sides, between our
wet ribs like the last insult of a sword. our blood the river,
the river our blood, i can't know or tell the difference
now. i'm into the belly of the curve of the gravel road,
into an ether of headlights fumbling thru the downpour
and the nowhere of the woods from the other side of the

near bridge. i'm blinded by their brightness and the black around us, by the rumen of the river and the rain at the ground. there is a voice behind the lights like something i remember, a story not mine, but told to me once. a voice i can only hear and can't understand, not in these woods, in this storm. nothing could make sense here, but the rain, straight faced and pounding down on me and surely the end of the earth and all of us.

i stop this side of the bridge and the river, the line of our land and somehow always his land and his, my feet in his boots. i won't walk any further, although i can't hear, it's best to keep to what's yours, what the old man would say. there's a fracture in the car lights, a man i think and close to the ground and bent with the rain, his shoulders round with the weight of the moment. he is part of the storm and its chaos, walking across the bridge like he's not sure of the ground or his good lord.

"mr. .... river .... help ....?"

i can only watch him, his words falling around me like the rain and into the ground where they'll never be heard, but grow into weeds come summer.

"mr. tully? ....tully's road? ...."

"i'm james, his son, my father's dead!"

our voices are vain and like all prideful things, humbled and eventually ruined by the storm. it seems a man and not some bit of my imagination, but some part of the dark that crosses the bridge. in the car lights i can see it's the little man, his clothes hanging around him, heavy with water and an impotent sadness. it seems the storm has broken his back, maybe his faith. he's a man that lives on faith, by the crucifix around his neck. he smells wet, of rain and human. the smell of the morning, of burnt toast and aftershave has washed away.

"kapelka? what the fuck are you doing out here?"
"mr. tully, i have your father."
"jesus christ, you scared the shit out of me, you could have brought us the ashes on monday."
"i don't have your father's ashes."
"you just said you did."
"mr. tully, i have your father's body still."
"what?"
"there's no power anywhere east of here, they say it's affecting the entire northeast and parts of canada, the radio says it was lightning, it sent a power surge thru the entire u.s. grid."
"jesus christ i figured it was local, just a downed line."
"the radio news is saying it's affecting millions of people, all

of new york, ohio, pennsylvania, michigan, it's incredible."

"so why didn't you leave his body at the crematorium?"

"i couldn't get to the highway without gas and there's no pumps because there's no electricity, i've been sitting at the station half way waiting for the power to come back, but it never happened, i finally siphoned some gas out of an old truck he's repairing there, i tried to get back to town, but the river road's flooded before the wood bridge."

"yeah, i know the river's flooding, but what do you want me to do?"

"mr. tully, this is your father, you have to ... i mean until the proper services and such are available again, you..."

"have to what? you want me to take the body?"

"well, yes."

"you're fucking nuts! what about your duty, what was all that talk about this morning?"

"mr. tully, please try to understand, i live in a very small house with my wife and two children, i can't get into town to the mortuary and i simply do not have room at my house for the deceased other than in the living room, if i don't hurry i won't be able to get home at all with the river rising ... my family needs me."

"why can't you just leave him in the hearse? it's not like he's going to know."

"mr. tully, i can't leave your father in the car in the garage."

"why not?"

"beside the fact that it's disrespectful, it's far too warm, remember your father's body wasn't prepared for viewing, he was going straight to cremation, he wasn't embalmed."

"fuck!"

"mr. tully, i know this is a difficult time for you, but we really don't have any choice."

"well why the fuck are you sitting out here in the woods?"

"i don't want to risk the bridge, it's shaking pretty good, the river is really pounding her."

"so what do we do?"

"we're going to have to carry the deceased by hand."

"it's like a goddamn mile to the house, kapelka! it's pouring rain, there's no electricity at the house, fuck! this is fucking crazy."

he's already walking towards the hearse, he's not the little man, he is john kapelka, he is a husband and a father and a father and a man full of faith. he is a believer like the river beneath him, beneath the bridge, something in the way his feet touch the ground. and what am i, but recycled matter and eventually something else, spots of carbon and hydrogen and oxygen atoms, the frayed strands of a soul, maybe, and mainly just space.

"mr. tully, please hurry, i need to get home, the river's rising every minute."

"sorry, i'm coming. i don't know... never mind, let's just get this done."

"the house has a cellar?"

"yeah, but we can't go down there, it's a mess."

"it can't be that bad, older people tend to hang onto things, i've seen it all in twenty three years, it will be fine, most importantly it's cool."

"god the bridge really is rocking."

"well it made it this far, with the grace of god it will hold a few more days."

"if the water doesn't get over the bridge i think it will be okay."

we're at the hearse, at its back doors, kapelka is next to me, but i feel i'm by myself, by my thoughts, i've been here before, ten hours ago. it feels like a week. everything is syrup, slowed down and at its edges, everything seems strangely clear and bone simple, night and a car's light, life and death. kapelka throws the doors open without the ceremony of the morning, he steps into the back like a nail drove into a plank, pure and purposeful. my father's body is there, a chore rather than a side show act, the rest of him in the cellar and ground into his chair. there are melted bags of ice on top of him, clear bags wrinkled with a blue polar bear and the word 'ice' printed across the bottom. all i can see of him is the calloused yellow bottoms of his otherwise livid feet.

"peter krysinski at the station gave me all the ice out of

their machine, it was just melting anyway, it was kind of
him though, he drives in to saint joseph's every sunday,
they're good people. i don't have anything to keep your
father dry, i'm sorry i wasn't prepared for this."
"here."

i let his slicker slide off me, off my arms like something
forgiven. i hand it to kapelka, maybe i toss it to him. the
rain feels cool on my shoulders, inevitable, honest after the
lie of waterproof. he lays the hood over my father's face,
the remainder draped over his torso. kapelka is soaked and
still in his suit jacket, the water dripping off his nose from
the wet chances of his thinning hair. he pushes the gurney
out of the hearse into the night. the drum of the rain on
the slicker shocks me like some sort of domestic betrayal.

"mr. tully take that end of the gurney please."

i can only do what he tells me, my head a loose bale of
wire, my thoughts wound around themselves until there's
nothing else, but myself. i can't seem to find my voice,
but a voice in my head screaming not even words, only a
racket clamor of blue and black and the old tin of pain i've
carried my whole life like a typhoid. i'm almost disgusted
like i've stepped in dog shit or ate a bad clam. this death
needs to be gone and not at the ends of my arms, death
all around me, and him and the dark and dead trees. i

can hear his voice again, kapelka saying something, i can only hear the rain or the hum of blood in my head or the river. i walk into the dark only knowing everything i ever knew was wrong.

11

we live thru every moment of our lives, i'm a little less because of it. i'm forty now and i'm wearing away and finally small enough to be a man, small enough to move on, maybe, from this world to the next. i sometimes think i died the night nikki said good bye, the night the old man died, memories i can only endure and live with like staying with a drunk lover. i wonder if i've been dead ever since, maybe a ghost dreaming soundless thru the apartment, thru the old square house, down the gravel road now. maybe i'm nothing more than the smoke of a blown out candle or a carryout coat wandering into the fog, eating chinese every night, reading fortune cookie fortunes for clues and all my dumb books over again. i almost can't remember her, just everything around her and the words "i love you, but i can't be with you" around her mouth, the way she folded her napkin, her fork in her left hand like they taught her. i still sleep on my side of the bed thinking i don't want to get in the habit of sleeping on her side. i pray that she's well, it's the least she could do for me and all i could ask. i wonder if she's kept my secrets, i haven't kept hers, but we both know i'm a son of a bitch.

i'll live and live with myself no matter how i try. i'll live with him and his old coffee can jangle, i have to, i only saw myself in his eyes. he is the quiet that comes over me, the thick rage that's corned in me, something not mine, but i own all the same, a faith without believing. his black sadness is on me like an oil stain, a bird trapped in tar and flapping its wings and never escaping. his blood has wrecked me and can't even kill me. he has crippled me and pushed me along. he is dead behind me and forever in front of me. i am a piece of him, more than i want to be. i am all of him that's left and a dry cough and the cellar and the broken chair in the shed.

and her there, faltered in the house there, humming her hymns, her candles burning, her prayers going up in tiny smoke. i can already hear her, i don't want to hear her, her rambling on that it's a sign from god and 'god's will and god bless... and at the hour of our deaths, amen'. i'm carrying a corpse home like a house cat with a mouse in its mouth, leave it on the porch, come take a look. this is her husband, my father, a part of the earth, a sashing if not a block. i wonder what his death is, what he was dreaming, what seared thru his mind in the last twitch, the breath before the last breath, life like a held breath, all of us always knowing we're going to breathe out. we forget. i hope he wasn't scared. i wonder if he was ready, really ready when his suicide came due.

kapelka's conversation is somehow wordless and like whistling, nervous habit to fill the lime cracks of the insanity around us, talk of embalming, the townies and the church goers, setting stones in the cemetery. i will only hear him years from now when i remember, but in this moment i am deaf to him. he is behind me, i am blind to him, my father behind me, the weight of him, my hands knuckled at the gurney's handle, my arms spent with fatigue so that i almost can't let go. it's all i can do to feel ahead hoping his boots might remember, squinting into the yellow worthless light barely ahead of this old battery rattle. i'm sure kapelka can't even see, but he knows where he's going, he believes.

i'm talking to nikki in my head, almost out loud, the hiss of the rain is too much for kapelka to hear me. i'm trying to tell her what's happening so i might know myself. i'm trying to tell her i'm sorry, but i won't, i can't let myself off that easy. i'm hoping someday, but i don't really believe, but disbelief is the matter of miracles. faith is burdened with expectation and expectation is the death of faith. i wonder if i'll ever kiss her again, if i can leave the lines alone and just listen. maybe this was all meant to happen, maybe sometimes someone has to die and the rest of us have to live.

i dream about her, i think, i wake when it's still night, but i never can quite keep her. it seems she's there walking thru my sleep, just a feeling i get like there's someone in the apartment or that i've been here before. i listen into the dark and the streetlight's fold into the room. i listen, but there's always some other sound, the first sound, before any other, the birth push of the morning before the ocean roar of the traffic, and the metal whir and the beat of the seams of the bay bridge, and the cable vein at chestnut and columbus, what doesn't start till six. it is the rattle of life, something between us, her and me, the string of chemistry, nylon or cat gut. it is the sound of the earth beginning and the grind of a whole universe spinning about its end. i listen, but it's nothing.

"mr. tully ... mr. tully ... james."

"what?"

"if you walk the opposite foot forward from me it will go much smoother."

"what?"

"just stop for a second."

i stop, i'm grinding my teeth, i can feel my anger wash thru me like all my blood has broke loose.

"kapelka let's go, i mean who fucking cares!"
"it will be far easier on us, otherwise we're not going to make it."
"i'll make it don't worry."
"i'm sure you will, but i don't think i will, please james, just start with your right, okay ... ready ... go."
"... sorry, man."

kapelka doesn't answer, he probably never heard me, i won't repeat it. it seems best not to, it seems better to be quiet now, to be inside ourselves, away from the rain and the black and the dead, everything we're afraid of at the ends of our elbows and over our knees. we head again into the spare beam of the flashlight like damned angels, but seemingly more efficient. my steps are clumsy with mud and the momentum of their unfamiliar weight, my shoulders are on fire, the pain so great i can't tell if i'm grimacing or smiling, all of it somehow satisfying and catholic. the rain is infinite, it has never started or stopped. i can hear his voice, i'm not sure if it's kapelka or my memory. he said james rather than tully, it was an appeal and nothing familiar. we will always be strangers and strangely bonded by this day, these first days of the old man's death and somehow the start of our own deaths.

i won't see the house, but i'll feel it like something between my teeth. we're half way from the near bridge, i don't know how i know, but i know, some part of my memory turned to marrow, something i don't use or have room to remember, but keep. i feel the gurney pull from behind me, kapelka has stopped. the rain is straight down, the dark muddled with darker trees.

"james, i have to stop, i'm sorry."

he's dropped his end, i hear him groan, maybe break. i crouch down and lower my part, my hands sinking into the gravel and a maternity of mud below that. the river is on the road, maybe an inch or inches, i didn't notice when we were walking. kapelka's face is like a coroner's photo in what light is left of the flashlight after the rain. he is colorless if not septic. maybe he's dying, maybe we're both dead, maybe this is the end of us and the beginning of hell.

"kapelka, you all right?"
"i don't know if i can go any further...
i need to rest for a moment...
i've never carried a body this far."

his words are broken apart by breaths, he's hunched over with his hands on his knees. he sounds like a hurdy gurdy, i can hear him praying, something davidian, how long lord, how long? i'm embarrassed to listen like his god might answer. i'm embarrassed to look holding the light on him like a broken circus performer. i don't know where else to turn the light. i turn my head instead.

"hey kapelka, it's cool, i could use a minute too, my arms feel like they're going to fall off, i've never carried a body this far either."

i try a laugh, i'm ridiculous, i sound like i'm talking to a dog. i'm talking so i don't have to hear his praying, almost praying myself to the voice in my head.

"james, i don't have anything left, i'm sorry."
"come on kapelka, you're a faith machine, man, you can make it."
"it's not a question of my faith, it's the body that's weak, i've reached my limit, james, i'm sorry, i... i don't know what to do."
"come on we'll rest when we need to, we can do this, let's give it another try."
"i can't."

he's fallen onto his knees, his back curved up, his body trying to vomit, but there's nothing, only choking dry heaves and his apologies between.

"oh fuck."

"i'm...huh...huh...huh... i'm sorry."

"it's all right."

"i don't... huh... huh... i don't know what to do."

"help me put the gurney up on its wheels, i'll drag it."

"i don't know if you can."

"what else am i going to do, kapelka, i can't leave my father's body here on the road."

"i can't leave you alone, here... i do have a duty."

"you've done your duty, get back to your family and i'll take care of mine, i'm fine, i've been on my own my whole life. just show me how to work this thing."

"i don't feel right about this."

"you've done enough ... everything you could, now it's my part, that's just the way it is ... kapelka? show me how to raise the gurney."

"the lever is here, help me lift it up, ready, one, two, three... lock it again here, okay... well does it move?"

"it's fine, take the flashlight, you're going to need it."

"see if the gurney will move."

"i told you i'm fine... see, we're moving. here's the flash-light, get going."

"i can't take the light."

"kapelka take the fucking flashlight, otherwise you're gonna wind up lost or in the river and i don't need to come find your sorry ass out here, i've got enough bullshit

to deal with, i don't need the light, i was born here."
"you're going to need the light."
"fuck it then, come on!"

i pull him into the beam of the flashlight, the old man's body behind us, we'll be at the near bridge in ten minutes on our own. i have my arm up and under his, dragging him along. he is lighter than i would think, a shoe box of bird bones. we won't speak, even my thoughts have stopped, the rain pouring down around us has brought everything to a silence. we will be timeless for this time in the storm, in the dark. we will only exist again in the door lights of the hearse like we were pushed out of the storm like a rain.

"you locked the doors? out here?"
"it's just habit, i'm sorry."

we sit down hard on the front seats, spent and wet like newborns.

"thank you, james, i'll be fine, you should get back to your father's body."
"yeah."
"i haven't seen the river like this since i was a boy."
"it flooded in '63."
"i think you're right."
"it was the year i was born, the old man used to talk about it."

"they rebuilt the wood bridge after that. we didn't have school for what seemed like a month, we had services at home, my father read at the mortuary chapel... i grew up in the mortuary."

"that must have been pretty weird."

"being raised in the mortuary?"

"well it's sort of twisted, i mean it sounds like a nightmare for a little kid."

"i never knew any different, it's a beautiful home, i'd live there with my family now, but my older brother is there with his wife and children, i'm fine with that, he's the first son."

"didn't you freak out as a kid with all those dead bodies around?"

"no, i think i grew up with a healthy understanding of death. it's our natural progression, barring accidents and even accidents are part of god's plan, they're only accidents from our small perspective."

"i just can't imagine death in my face every day."

"it's around all of us every day, people just choose to ignore it, you're dying, we both are, right now."

"i'd like to think that i'm living and not dying."

"if you live your life with god, you won't die, you'll pass judgment and pass on, you'll live forever."

"do you really believe that?"

"i do."

"i've made so many mistakes..."

"we all do, our lives are made of mistakes, we learn from

them and pray we can do better, god is forgiving, people too, forgiving ourselves is the hard part."

i look at my reflection in the windshield, at the black behind that, i can't look at him when he talks about god. it's like he's talking about having sex with his wife, something too intimate to look someone in the eye and listen. i look down at my feet, i can't even bear to see myself.

"i'm sorry to put you thru all this, i wasn't prepared for anything like today."

"you don't have to be sorry, it's not you, it's them, it's him, it's my mother, everything they touch turns into some sort of chaos."

"i must admit i was a bit shocked when i came to get your father's body yesterday morning, it's a shame your mother had to live in such conditions."

"oh fuck her, she's a party to it. no one had a gun to her head."

"she's a good woman, james, she deserved better."

"she could have cleaned the house, picked up, thrown things out. hell, she could have left if she wanted, everyone thinks she's some kind of martyr, believe me she's no martyr, she's a selfish bitch, she just hid away in church rather than in a bottle. either way it was all just a cop out."

"your mother has a very deep faith."

"my mother is full of shit, she's a coward, it's all a way

to avoid the truth, and the truth is she abandoned her husband and her child for god, because god didn't tell her anything she didn't want to hear."

"we all have our means to carry our burdens, you handled things your way, your mother put her faith in god."

"you want to know about burdens, let me tell you... i'm like seven or something, a little kid, i have to come home from school every day to an empty house, except this one day her car's in the driveway. i'm thinking she's surprising me with cookies or some shit, so i run up the gravel road and i open the back door and the faucet's running and i find her on the kitchen floor in a pool of blood, she's lying there and i can't wake her up. i run outside to get help like a dumb kid, christ, i'm fucking seven years old. of course there's no one for miles and i'm standing there and then this kind of quiet comes over me and everything slows down and i walk back into the house, turn the faucet off, sit down and call the sheriff. i sit in my father's kitchen chair till they get there, a deputy first, probably twenty minutes later, then the ambulance. i could hear their sirens way off, one then the other, and their tires on the gravel road. i just sat and waited, i was outside my body almost, like i was watching the whole thing, watching myself. sometimes i don't think i ever came back, you know, sometimes i feel like i've been watching my whole life happen since, like everything's wrapped in cellophane and i can't quite touch it. i couldn't tell if she was still alive or not, if she was breathing, i held my breath and listened the whole time i was waiting. i sat there and stared at her blood, i was fascinated with it, it was red and almost brown like the river mud. i stared into it like a mirror, i can still see my reflection in it like an old photo or something you remember. when the deputy came in he knelt down next to her and looked back at me and told me that maybe i should go outside. i looked over my shoulder as i was going out the back door and the deputy was blowing into her mouth. i went down and looked in at the police cruiser, the shot gun and the cage between the front and back seats, the radio was saying something, i didn't know what the word meant, but i knew our address. my father was coming back from the river along the gravel road here when he saw the sheriff's car and the ambulance. he went straight up and down, but his face didn't change. he ran past the shed, past me and in the kitchen still holding onto the day's samples. they took her in the ambulance to the city hospital, we followed her in the old man's truck, i held onto the sample bottles and he tried to keep up. she was in the hospital for three weeks. the old man drank all day and slept in his chair every night she was gone. she came home in pajamas and a robe and she thanked god and never said a word to me. neither of them spoke of it, ever."

"what happened?"

"she'd been pregnant. they say she miscarried and hemorrhaged."

"dear god."

"that's the official report. i think she did it to herself."

"you can't say that."

"i saw things, things i shouldn't have seen, in the sink and the faucet running and all, but that's my burden, right?"

kapelka can only look at me like i'm some retarded boy who pissed himself on the bus, his face raked with compassion and contempt. i'm angry that i told him, i'm angry that i remembered, that i can't forget. i don't know why i told him, i need someone to know the truth. there was only them and me, but he won't listen, no one listens, really, we already know whatever we're going to know and never hear any different.

"i'll come by when there's a break in the rain, i pray the bridge holds."

"it'll hold, it held in '63, it'll hold thru this."

"god help us."

"help yourself, man and get going."

"james, your mother and father raised a good man."

"the hell with them."

i say it like i would say good bye to a hotel clerk, matter of factly and final. i close the car door, i don't look back, the car lights sweeping across the trees and the fabric of the rain as he turns the hearse around. then there is only the flashlight beam bouncing like a lightening bug between the trees and the notion of me somewhere behind it until i have become only a thought, something that seems real and is really nothing.

his body is in the gravel road like a disease, like his nightly tantrums, his morning tremor and twitch. i grab onto the gurney and lean back with all my weight and the lead weight of a lifetime. the gurney moves a few feet and i lean back and pull it again. the wheels are dug in, but they're sliding if they're not rolling. i turn the flashlight off and wedge it in my father's armpit, my back to the road, the little light is useless. i continue to row my father back, the rain seems to have lessened or i've grown immune, i can't be sure. i'm into a rhythm, i'm unconscious, pure existence, stayed to the road between the trees each side of me, a tittle-tattle i can barely make out from the sky. i can feel the gravel though, the river hasn't made it here yet, the gravel road rising to the house on a rise above a stretch of hollows and high enough so far.

i have no idea how long i've been out here, i've never felt like i've known less. i'm in the big black of god, maybe the belly of a whale or the great northern pike that haunts the lake. the old man knew it like a dream, said he saw it as a boy and he never saw it again, but for something big moving the water. he swore it followed him since, maybe it's following me. i saw its shadow once beneath our old aluminum boat. i was just in the wee part of my memory, my shadow in the water too, the sun behind me. and for a moment it swam right thru me and i felt the cold of the bottom of the lake and i knew right then how i must die, better than i would ever know how to live. i haven't forgot and stay close to shore and yet always near the water. we're drawn to our deaths like broken men to the women who will break us, something we both know is no good, but satisfies some dark thirst we inevitably can't cool.

no one seems to know me now. i am without her and strangely without him even with his rind at the end of my arms. i am like a building stripped of its ivy, bare bricks where i used to be. maybe this is my chance to finally see, to look hard at myself and what they left me. it's hard to look, it seems impossible to change, yet everything chang-es, different waters downstream. i'm broken, i can see that, goddamned busted but good, but i've been broken before and grown back, crooked maybe, but bones grow back stronger at the break. it's the rest that worries me.

i can make out the grim whisper of her seven day candles thru the windows from over my shoulder, the whole house some broken down altar. i'm at the front porch steps, i don't know how. i have to rest before i take him in the house, four steps up to the front door and the steps down into the cellar. the gurney wheels are packed with mud, i doubt they'll roll. i'll leave him in the rain and lie here on the porch floor for a few minutes more till i'm ready. my skin hurts from the rain or without it. my body is ruined with the day and this first part of the night. the porch roof is leaking, there's a large puddle on the floor boards, the floor boards nearly rotted away, gray like dead skin, twisting off of the square nails that have held them for so long. the rain pounds on the old man's slicker and the old man, reminding me that neither the rain nor i am done. it's good friday and his body is home.

12

she spit me out into the world, into the weather, and whether it was a monday night or a march it doesn't matter, that push alone makes her my mother. she's all i have now, some part of my superstition, something i'm afraid to not need, my last shard of family, my last root before my tree tumbles into the river. and maybe my water is muddy, but in time everything the world's done to me and everything i've done to myself will settle to the bottom of me and i'll be able to see and see my feet and who i was in the beginning, something perfect, perfectly. then i'll be free if not alone and have time to think and maybe even know something if only the clarity of clean water.

her, she's what's left of her parents' marriage, her father's red hair, his irish chin put out, the coil of her french mother's tongue, her small mouth and small eyes that felt something like a switch. my mother's eyes are green and don't work, but for glasses and a right eye that doesn't work at all, what remains of her childhood and a brother's toy arrow. she'd look to her left and squint and see the world she wanted to see, keeping reality to her right and to god's hands. she'd marry my father and start it all over, that's all i know, but we never know our mothers, their lives like the bottoms of their purses, secret and cluttered and someplace we'd never dare look.

everywhere there's candles burning, burned down from before, ten thousand prayers like birthday wishes, lit since yesterday, since they carried the old man's body away. they're only conspicuous amongst the clatter because there's no other light, blue and green saints with bare white feet, six red wax madonnas. there's a jesus on the marble topped table, her mother's prized possession, him wrecked and beautiful beneath a crown of thorns, the flame behind his face like the bright idea of life. her voice is in the kitchen, everything happened in the kitchen, everything forgotten and never forgotten, but remembered only as an inexplicable ache.

"mom?"
"james, i'm in here, anne bender called to see if i was all right, she's saying the radio said that we might not have

power for days, it's the entire northeast, detroit, cleveland, buffalo, even new york city, they're saying it was lightning, but ron thinks it was terrorists."

"who's ron?"

"you know ron, ron bender, ann's husband."

"i don't, it doesn't matter."

"they've been at saint joseph's since you were baptized."

"mom, i have to..."

"i'm on the phone with ann still, sweet heart."

"jesus christ."

"eat the pork before it goes bad, i think the ham will be okay, ann do you think the ham is okay out like that? james, the jello's melted, but there's sauerkraut."

"mom!"

"what darling?"

"i need to talk to you now, maybe you could call your friend back."

"ann, james needs something, let me call you back... of course, well if saint joseph's is open sunday i'll be there... oh we're fine, ben has enough food in the freezer for a year, if we don't eat it it will just go bad... i don't know, i should call her, with all the excitement around here i forgot all about her ... dear god don't tell her ... well why don't you call her i still have so many details to work out for ben's memorial... she's been feeling poorly, i don't think she's been in church for two weeks..."

"mom! please."

"ann, i have to go... he's just like his father, i've never known a man to have any patience... he came in from california last night... as soon as he heard... no, he drove in from the airport in some funny little rental car, it's cute... well that morning i'm planning on ..."

"i give up."

i walk back outside, the rain feels familiar, almost good, i'd forgotten how hot it is, it's even hotter in the house, the same spoiled air he breathed and didn't breathe. his body is there, out in the rain, it's not a shock anymore, maybe a dull pain, a sprain that will turn arthritic, but nothing more. i don't think i'll ever know how weird this day was, how could i? how can i remember a lifetime and remember today. my memory colored inside the lines and all my life just scribble. all this just a story in the end, paper thin instead of thick, small enough to fit on a page when it didn't even fit into a life. this flesh and blood once is just an abstraction now, a spasm across my brain, someplace in space where everything is always, but that's for an einstein to decide, some stephen hawking in his chair, not me.

i can hear the bland of her chatter, her hokum and hooey, the tatter of the rain song and a song that's stuck in my head. some damn tune i can sing but i can't say, something saved for midnight radio, ella fitzgerald or elvis costello i think. i stick my tongue between my teeth and bite down and pull the gurney with a rage i save for occasion. i can feel the wood steps bending with my effort so i think they might break, the gurney wheels give and turn enough to get the old man's body onto the porch. i don't squander my momentum or my anger and pull his body thru the front door, the screen door scraping against the gurney, the wood door smashing into the plaster wall, the knob settling into an old hole, the door stop long gone. we're rolling down the hall to the cellar past a candle madonna willow armed and open and the accepting stare of the jesus on the side table next to the t.v..

"james? ... oh my god!"
"i was trying to tell you, but you can't get off the phone for even a minute."
"oh my god!..."
"kapelka couldn't get him to the crematorium because of the power failure, there's no gas and he can't get back to the mortuary because of the river flooding, he was afraid to even cross the near bridge, the river's really running hard, i had to drag dad all the way down the gravel road."
"my darling ben, oh my god, my darling ben ..."

she's pulled the slicker off his face, she's kissing him, his forehead and his blue lips, she's wiping the rain from his cheeks and jaw, cooing darling ben over again and smoothing his hair down, a great gray and gunmetal wisp i'm just noticing, his hair as thick as any twenty year old's. i continue to the cellar door as she shuffles along the side like an overwhelmed fan. i'm sick with her, i can't watch, it's like watching her eat with her mouth open, like they're having sex, an intimacy that's frantic if not inappropriate, ridiculous and probably dire.

"your father wouldn't let me kiss him on the lips since he started losing his teeth, he only had one or two teeth left in the end, he was so embarrassed, i mean his breath was rotten and he'd burp up his food all night because he couldn't chew his food right, he kept saying he was going to go down to the sears and roebucks and get dentures, it's all the sugar in that damn booze, it just rotted his teeth away, it rotted all of him away, i'm sure. don't think that he didn't provide his husbandly duties though, your father and i had a ..."

"jesus mom! please i don't want to hear about it."

"well for forty two years i was a very happy woman, your father and i were both virgins when we married, it was a little awkward at first, but your father was so patient with me, he..."

"mom stop! please, i'm begging you, i can't listen to this... ah shit, i forgot there's no lights, you're going to have to hold the flashlight on the steps for me... you have to go down ahead of me."

"oh james, i can't go down there, that's your father's

workshop, i can't go down there, i can't, you're the man in the family now, it's a man's space, your father would've wanted you to go down there."

"mom, please i can't see a thing."

"you know you're right you should do what you want with his things, i shouldn't let the boys down until you say it's okay."

"mom, try to take a breath and relax, okay. i need you to hold the flashlight on the steps for me so i can get dad into the cellar, it's cooler down there.

"i can't go down there, i've ... i can't."

"mom?"

"i have to call theresa, maybe the boys can help you."

"mom, you can't expect someone to come out to the house in this weather and with the river over its banks, just relax, okay. i'm right here, dad's right here, this is between us, this is family, okay?"

"i can't believe your father's in the house again, i didn't think i'd ever see him again."

"mom, it's not really him, it's just sort of a… shell."

"he's at peace now, you're right, james, my darling ben is at peace. i didn't want you to see him like this, he was ... i wanted him cremated before you got here so you wouldn't have to see what happened to him, i wanted you to remember him down by the river when he was young, when you were young, but he looks at peace, don't you think?"

"sure mom, he looks fine."

"my darling ben..."

his mouth is naked, agape, ghastly black, a hole that still resonates with anger, an only child's rancor, maybe the voice in my head. i'm afraid to look for i might never look away, like i've met my maker and i'll burn if i dare even glance into him. his eyes are closed, but they might as well be open, i can feel them smoldering beneath his heavy lids. one with a small growth, a pebble of skin that makes him look like some perverse version of him, of what i remember. he is unmaintained, ruined, he is twisted and pulled, a tree torn from the ground by a great wind, its roots in the air, his death unnatural, purposeful. he has done this to himself, what life didn't do. he drank himself into a darkness, a forgetfulness and finally the relief of nothingness. he was done with this life and he went raging from it and if i listen i can hear him, the blunt object of his voice, repeating and repeating.

"mom, mom? i need you to pull yourself together, okay."
"i'm fine, it's just a shock, i didn't think i'd ever see your father again and here he's come home."
"mom, we need to put dad in the cellar, we have to get him someplace cool, okay?"
"he really does look at peace james. he was a good man, he was, he loved you, boy, he talked about his son in cali-fornia all the time, he was very proud of you, he told me

how proud he was, how good you turned out."

"yeah, well it's hard to believe anything he said, he was always half smashed."

"he had his moments, james. your father was a very sensitive man, he struggled, but he was a good man, i wouldn't have stayed with him otherwise."

"why did you?"

"i loved your father dearly and he loved me, he took good care of me."

"what are you talking about, look at this place, the house is in shambles, the whole place is a monument to insanity. you've lived in this craziness for so long you don't even know what normal is anymore."

"i don't spend all my time here, i knew your father was sick, james. alcoholism is a disease, there's nothing your father could have done."

"you didn't spend any time here, but we've been thru this bullshit a thousand times, i don't buy it, any of it, he had a choice, just like you had a choice, but let's just drop it. i just want to get him in the cellar and get dried off and go to sleep. i'm not going to get into some big thing tonight, i don't have the energy."

"your father didn't have a choice, he was an alcoholic, his father was an alcoholic, your uncles. my father was until he went and got the cure, that's what they called it in those days."

"bullshit."

"it's true, i couldn't have been much more than five or six. he went away for three weekends in a row and he never drank again once they were done with him. he told me years later, that it was the most terrible thing that ever happened to him, that he'd rather die than go back."

"grandpa still drank."

"james, he did not, he never drank again."

"i don't remember much of him, but i remember him giving me sips of whiskey from the flask he kept in his jacket pocket when we went fishing."

"james david tully!"

"he said an irishman always has a bit before they fish, for luck and good spirits, that it was our secret, between men and he'd go into one of those stories of his about the lake or some storm or the great northern pike and have a few more tastes. god i hated it, but it felt like magic, it was worth tasting like medicine if it was magic. that was like six in the morning or something, mom, you can't tell me he wasn't drinking the rest of the day."

"well i never knew anything about it."

"of course not, nothing ever happened around here. everyone in this family is in denial, probably even me."

"i've been in alanon for almost twenty years..."

"come on, we know, don't we mom? deep down in our guts. that we're full of shit, both of us.

"so you think you're full of it?"

"the only thing i know is that i don't know a damn thing.

there must be something wrong with me, i'm not happy, every relationship i've been in has ended in complete ruins, i'm either choosing fucked up people or i'm fucked up or both. neither one is a good thing. i know nikki's a good person and we had a good thing and we wrecked it somehow, i wrecked it and i don't know how...but i know, i guess, i just can't face it."

"you're a good man, i never liked the sound of her."

"you don't like her because she could see right thru you and your superficial crap, even on the phone she knew you were full of shit."

"i flew all the way out to san francisco to meet her and she was very cold with me."

"no she just didn't kiss your ass."

"i don't like the way she treated you, she was very aloof from what i saw, she was a very conflicted young woman."

"i can't talk to you about this, you're just defending me because this is all some threat to you and your fucked up idea of reality, it's always about you."

"how's this about me?"

"well, how can your son be fucked up unless you're fucked up. that's what nikki saw in you, this narcissistic shit that you cover up with your phony caring talk and all your talk about god and jesus and whatever... she helped me see what you're really all about."

"so you've made mistakes, we all have, including me, i know i'm not perfect."

"it's not just some mistake, i'm doing real damage to people... damage to myself."

"james, you have so many beautiful qualities."

"there's nothing beautiful about any of it, i'm fucked up and angry at... i'm angry at i don't even know what... everything. i hate him... and i hate you."

"you get out of this house!"

"believe me the first chance i get, i will."

"i had a long talk with nicole today, she thinks you need help."

"don't talk to me about getting help, you don't even know me!"

"of course i know you, you're my flesh and blood."

"that's all you know, you were never here, you left me here with a fucking drunk every night because you couldn't take it."

"don't you use that language in this house. i had to listen to it for forty two years and i won't listen to it anymore."

"and what makes you think i could listen to it, i was a little kid."

"your father did the best he could."

"i'm not talking about him, i'm talking about you! where the fuck were you? at god damn church choir."

"i endured your father so you could have a mother and a father."

"that's a bunch of shit, you stayed with him because you're as fucked up as he was."

i'm not listening to you when you talk like this."

"you're going to listen, you can't run off to church tonight."

"james, is this what you're learning from this therapist person? anna laura."

"it's hannalore. i suppose nikki told you about that, too."

"you need to put your faith in god, james. let go, let god, that's what we say at alanon."

"more clichés, thank you, what would i do without you."

"well if you think that's all i've ever done for you, let me tell you something james david tully, i think i was a pretty good mother, you certainly had it better than i did growing up."

"oh my god, you are completely delusional. my childhood was a circus sideshow... come see the bottomless man drink a gallon of bourbon, the disappearing woman, the only child the freak."

"i don't think you're funny."

"neither do i."

"i will not discuss this in front of your father."

"he's dead! for once open your eyes."

"i don't know where all this anger is coming from."

"look the fuck around, you're living in it."

"you can't dwell on the past, james."

"fuck you!"

"now i know why nicole left you."

i push his body down the cellar steps, down into the black where the candle light won't reach, down into the earth

where this death belongs. i'm grieving the recklessness of
it as i do it, my trick inhibition, my whim and wiggle, the
crack and schism of the moment before i let go when i
could've still held on. i almost have to do it, i don't have a
choice, i read the last page of this twisted book first. i'll do
what i do whether i want to or not. i'm as helpless as any
river to be anything other than the rain that fell before it.
i am the rage of him, the blind eye of her, nikki's taciturn,
the green apples in the yard, what the birds don't eat and
what they swallow and shit on the car. there's an awful
moment of silence before the gurney hits the first step,
her gasp, and the sound of metal and the subtler sound
of his corpse catapulting down the stairs, the imaginable
concussion and conclusion and the awful silence again. she
can only skelter and scuttle, totter down the hall befuddled,
she won't say a word. her busy bang rattle in the kitchen,
silverware in the sink and water, maybe a cup and a sau-
cer and a silence between, the uneasy quiet of regret and
my creak on the stairs, up the stairs to my old room and
everything like nothing ever happened.

13

the days are growing longer now, the sun sooner in the morning, the morning thru the tangle of the trees. i take a certain solace in that, an odd satisfaction i can never quite explain, but we need secrets somehow, even from ourselves. i dreamt last night, i know it, i'm sure i dreamt of her. i won't remember, i never do, but i'll feel her on my skin like a day's work, like the myrrh of her sex, like her long hair across my face and my pillow. nik always had long hair.

there is a quiet below the usual silence, the rain has finally quit, but it's gray. it seems it will rain again, a different rain, the air has grown cold from a canadian front moving across the lake. you can smell the smell of water, of fish and the petroleum of fishermen's clothes. i get up and out of my old bed, my knees and ankles crack instead of bending, i'm forty, but it seems more, not so much the years as the mileage. i crank the bedroom windows closed like old bones, the house is freezing. yesterday it was eighty five, this morning it's probably not fifty, the uncertainty of seasons at their edges, of long northern winters and great lake springs.

his body is in the root cellar, i haven't forgotten. she's in her room downstairs breathing, novenas coming out of her sleep, out of the holes in her head. i slip into clean jeans, a t-shirt and a sweater, i packed for any weather, i knew to be ready, i grew up here. it feels like winter, the air thin where it was heavy just yesterday. i'm closing all the windows upstairs, their room and the bathroom. i head downstairs, down the toy steps into the morning after, into the smell of wax and dust and the smell of old people, sanguine perfume just above the decay. i have to see to her and to his body. i walk soft past her room, she's still sleeping. i close her door, but not all the way so i don't wake her. it's best not to wake her. i walk down the hall past the cellar door to the kitchen, the ham's there on the kitchen table still, i'm starving, i don't remember when i ate last. i grab three slices, it's already sliced, some store bought spiral sliced honey baked ham. it's sticky with brown sugar glaze and honey i suppose. i shove what i can into my mouth as i head down into the cellar, the slices flapping on my chin like a big tongue, a still burning seven day candle in each of my hands for light.

"jesus christ."

i breathe to myself thru the ham stuffed in my mouth. the gurney is on its side just at the bottom of the steps. everything about him seems unnatural, his torso and arms twisted like the old apple trees along the road that his father planted, his right leg bent backwards just below his knee. i marvel at the bone sticking thru his wax paper skin, what is that? his tibius maybe, tibia?

"fuck."

i wince and whistle. there's barely any blood, broken skin, his bones snapped like dry branches, something mannequin that hardly seems real, maybe the architecture of a higher power, maybe tissue paper and chicken wire. i right the gurney with an effort, taking concentrated breaths thru my nose and holding the slabs of ham still hanging out of my mouth with my lips so i don't bite thru and lose them. i feel like i'm ten again and i broke the green glass lamp playing basketball in the house. his leg is almost broken off, his shoulder dislocated, his right side in a permanent shrug. he would have hated it, it makes him look like he doesn't know. he always knew.

i know i have to try to put him back together again, all the kings horses and all the kings men, but he's a mess. surely the crematorium must be used to such things, farming

accidents and factory mishaps, cars and trucks and motor-
cycle crashes, our lives filled with an endless list of modern
things to tear us apart. and what if kapelka notices? there's
probably some law about abusing a corpse or some shit.
that little officious son of a bitch would probably turn
me in too. well fuck him he abandoned the body, he was
derelict in his duty, his solemn duty.

"fuck him."

i'm chewing the last of the ham in my mouth as thoughts
of my trial defense roll thru my head. i bolt the last bit
and breathe in deep and out.

"all right james... let's do this."

i'm looking for some bit of death around him, some tell
tale shadow or stench, but he is only lifeless, an empty
bucket, finally free of the burden of god's friction and
this life. he must be relieved, i am. this is the end of this.
this is the start of something ancient, some ritual, a right
i can only know in the earliest part of my stem. this is his
death, my life, the end of the river before i ever knew its
start, but we never know our fathers as men, we only know
them as ourselves.

i grab his ankle hard and just above his knee with my other
hand, i'm putting his leg straight, he's so stiff i'm afraid he

might break. there's tendon and bone crackling like i'm pulling a chicken wing away from a breast. i'm biting down on my tongue so i can almost taste blood and yet there's a part of me that's merely watching, detached, all of it a little too much to really absorb. his leg is out of plumb, his knee straight up, his shin and foot twisted away to his right. there's nothing to hold his lower leg in line, no bone or notion. i'm trying to push his shoulder down, it won't move, his collar bone sticking up into his neck. i cross his arms over his chest, but they will hardly bend, it seems like something i've seen before. it's all wrong, but it's the best i can do. i notice that i'm shaking, i didn't notice before.

"dad... i'm sorry... i..."

i can't push the words up, they're there and they'll stay there, somewhere deep down in my gut, some dark place where all my gravel sits. it's another moment of my life that i won't remember, there's no way to remember this. i'll make it up later, some story i'll tell myself until it's the truth. it's beginning to rain again, i can hear it above me, softly and insidious so only the soaked ground will notice.

"you'll be okay here."

i search for wood and knock on my head instead. i grab the candles at their tops from his work bench without thinking, my fingers seering to their sides.

"mother fucker!"

i drop the saint joseph, a little saint theresa, their light long
enough to see them shatter on the floor. my eyes recover
to the bare charity of the small window at the ceiling
just above the ground. i find the steps and shuffle up like
some tragic miner, his holes all filled with black, leaving
my father's body amongst the rest of his junk, stacks of
newspapers and scrap wood, rusting paint cans and an old
band saw. i try the lights at the top of the stairs and then
the kitchen lights out of habit, but there is only the dark.
the whole house is dead and gray from the thin light of
the new storm and yellow in the candles she's left lit like
dull aches.

an insult of water runs down the front of the refrigerator
and onto my feet and the floor as i open the freezer door.
i'm wet again, fuck it. i leave the puddle sadly on the
linoleum, the plywood beneath showing thru where the
flooring's been worn away. the freezer space is crammed
with t.v. dinners and ice cream cartons and cans of frozen
orange juice and meat and organ mysteries wrapped in
plastic and old margarine containers filled with leftovers.
everything is melted, all of it seems worn and years old.
i grab a thawed box of steak-ums from the freezer, god
knows how old they are, it's still cold enough to relieve the
pain of my burnt fingers for a while. i sit down in front
of the ham, my wet foot prints behind me, and shove

another slice into my mouth, chewing and holding the plastic wrapped mass of gray steak matter with both hands like you'd hold a wet baby at a baptism. i'm reading the side of the box, a potion of science and modern convenience, the expiration date seven years ago. i feel my blood push into my stomach, i feel like i might be sick, it's all too much, somehow more disturbing than the old man's body in the basement, everything in this house past its due date.

i look back at my footprints to check if i'm still here and at the rain just on the water that's collected in the ruts in the gravel road, a drizzle that is otherwise imperceptible thru the dirty windows. i think it might never stop, any of it, but it will. the last two days have taught me that and yet i wonder if i might stop first.

i bring my stare back inside. i'm watching the phone, waiting for it to ring, waiting til it's late enough to call the west coast, thinking what i might say, all the things i've said i wish i never said. i've waited my whole life, i'm not even sure for what. i waited for him to quit, to finally stop the boozing and the banging around, for everything to be okay, they said everything would be okay, the dirty cupboard below the phone like a broken new year's promise.

i was waiting for him to die, this life had to kill us and now he's dead and rotting in the cellar like the thawed meat in the freezer and more a part of my life than when he was alive. i'm waiting for nik to come home like i waited for her to come home, him screaming where is she, god damn church or choir group, god damn. but she never came home, not really, not the way i wanted or needed, neither one of them, my tiny breaths on the window till i couldn't see out, till i could only see myself.

14

i'll always be an only child, oily odds and ends of a mother and a father, remnants of them like the comet's old engine parts piled in a pop bottle crate on a board shelf in the shed, a car he drove into the ground years ago. i'll be all that's left of them, a voice on the phone or in my head, an echo of him coming out of my mouth. i can hear him when i'm angry, when i hate myself, when i've had too much to drink. but anger is something to taste, something to swish around in your mouth and swallow, something ugly and awkward and strangely beautiful. i am james tully and many things and always the son of them, a son of a bitch and a bastard. james is my mother's voice, "james david", the old man never seemed to say it. "james" is her in the morning, the lace of her across my leg like some dream i'm sleeping, her skin all my penny wishes and fingers crossed and only a moment, i sleep alone now. james is jimmy, the guys at work and somehow profane when they say it like everything they say. james is them, all of them and just a name and not me. and i'm on a bus home, the 45 and it's six o'clock crowded and buzzing with the mishmosh of kearny street and a chinese stockton and all the peoples and their red stinking bags of fish and their coats and shrugs and far east smells and somehow i'm alone still in the middle of all of them and this. i'm alone now, sitting at the kitchen table like a king before a wasteland, my mother sleeping still, still wrapped around her nighttime prayers. it's just me and this voice, what i hear when i listen or when i try not to listen.

it's morning and everything is only starting, his death and some part of my death, some part of the night and nik still in my eyes. somehow i don't know her anymore and i was inside her just months ago. i never knew her, how could i? i couldn't know myself, but i loved her like i didn't have a choice, and her, she loved me like she did, like i was a broken old hotel room, but a place to stay. i can't say i'm sorry, but i'm sorry. i know i didn't love her the right way, but i love her the right way. so many mistakes i've made, so much pain i've drawn, i'm not sure there's a way back.

i wonder if she thinks of me, who her next man will be, some italian probably with skinny legs and armani pencil pants. fuck... i wonder where she's sleeping, it's seven-thirty, it's four-thirty there, the oven clock chanting three-twenty-two like it always will. my mother says that's the time the old man passed away, but i don't believe her, i never believe her when she crosses herself. and who but the faithless will believe me and my story? i don't even believe it anymore.

i pick up the phone like it's the last call, maybe it is the last call. i start to dial her cell, but dial mine instead. i enter my code, the recording date of a love supreme, ...don't ask.

"you have three new voice messages, first new voice message sent yesterday..."
"jimmy, it's chrisman, we all heard what happened, every-one down at the shop's real sorry, you need anything, man, you got it, all right. take it easy, bro."
"end of message, to erase this message press ..."

i hit seven and squeeze out a hope that i'll hear her voice.

"next voice message sent yesterday."
"hey jimmy, scotty, i got work for you saturday, an iron gate up on a house on telegraph hill, it's one of those historical pieces of shit, your specialty, i really need you on this, my regular iron guy can't handle it. call me back, i can bill you out at four hundred for the day, maybe even five, i'll tell 'em you're catholic, it's probably only five or six hours work, they want it done before easter, call me back."

"end of message, to erase this ..."
"next voice message sent yesterday."

there is only the sounds of traffic, consequences of inertia and the mill of people and machines. some collective
sound of san francisco, a bass line that could be no other
city, a song of fog and the bay and the bay bridge you
must know to live there. i listen and wait for a voice, for
something to be said ...

"end of message, to erase this message press seven, to
repeat it press one, to save it press..."

the conclusion of silence is we fill it with noise, with the
poison of prayers and worn soft dreams cotton in our
heads, but it's our hard cidered fears that we listen to, what
we keep in our spines, what we finally believe. i press one
and listen again and imagine i can hear her, her life wove
thru the life of the city and again and maybe her string
instead of the music, her blood like the rain water under
the street. i'll listen to it again and again until i can only
hear myself and the true silence of heartbreak.

"end of message, to erase this message press seven, to
repeat it press one, to save it press nine..."

"james? james is someone on the phone?"

she walks in pretending not to intrude. i have my hand over my eyes, i don't want her to see me, she won't see me. i'm staring down at the phone, at the digit nine, my finger presses down on the seven, a tone to a voice mail computer somewhere that it's over, but it won't stop until i do. i'm afraid to let my finger up like it's the last part of nik i'll ever hold.

"james, are you on the phone?"
"no."
"are you calling someone?"
"no."
"what are you doing? dear."
"mom, i'm checking my god damn messages, is that okay?"

i pull my finger away, it is the sound of black, the static air of the end.

"yes that's fine, james, of course, did you hear from nicole? maybe i shouldn't ask."
"no."
"no, she didn't call or no, i shouldn't ask."
"either."
"did you have breakfast already?"
"yeah i had steak and eggs and some hash browns, oh, and some of that delicious cherry pie you made for dessert last night."

"james, don't be so smart all the time. i'm well aware that i'm not a cook, but there's plenty of things to eat, people went to a lot of trouble for us."

"well come on mom, sit down and have some melted jello and fruit cocktail."

"i happen to love jello."

"i'm sure you do."

"i do, maybe we don't have all your fancy california taste here, but people here at home still appreciate simple delicacies."

"delicacies? it's green jello, mom, with a can of fruit cocktail poured into it."

"well you loved it when you were a child, you'd beg me to make jello."

"i begged you to make god damn anything, there was never anything to eat that wasn't a t.v. dinner or cereal, i was always starving."

"orange jello and strawberry, you loved strawberry, you'd play blocks with the jello and pudding boxes on the kitchen floor waiting for it to cool in the fridge. tapioca pudding, remember how you loved tapioca pudding?"

"whatever, mom."

"so what are your plans for today? i'm going to take the car and help father ciolek and the sisters with the easter prep at saint josephs."

"you're crazy, the river road's flooded."

"the rain's let up some, i'll call alan and judy they live by the wood bridge, see what they say, it should be fine."

"nothing's fine! your husband's body is in the cellar. why's it so god damn important for you, that no matter what, you go to church? why? can't you talk to god right here? i'm serious, what is it about church that you're so obsessed about, i mean you're beyond any common sense."

"my faith is my first priority, james."

"that's my point, it was always your first priority, over dad and me, over everything. there was never any mistake about that."

"that's because you don't understand the power of god. the only life that matters in the end is our spiritual lives."

"no, i don't understand how a mother picks a fable over her own flesh and blood."

"god is not a fable and i've never felt like i was choosing one over the other."

"bullshit, you chose to spend your time with god instead of us, instead of me."

"that's not true, i read to you every night before you went to bed."

"that's a lie."

"i read that doctor seuss book to you, oh what was the name of that book that you loved so much?"

"you can read a doctor seuss book in ten minutes and anyway, i have no memory of you reading to me ever. if you read to me every night i think i'd remember. most nights dad took me up to bed, that's what i remember.

he'd watch me put on my pajamas and i'd tell him i had to brush my teeth and he'd say goodnight and go back downstairs and scream at the t.v. and then at you when you finally got home."

"i think i was home before you went to bed."

"your entire life is just this story you make up in your head. mom, listen, i know you had a tough time of it with dad. nobody knows better than me, but you need to see what you did and what you did to me."

"i did what i thought was best for everybody."

"i don't see how leaving me with this drunk all night by myself was the best thing."

"your father was a good man, a brilliant man, he loved you, he would have never done anything to hurt you."

"he did a lot to hurt me and so did you, that's what you don't see or want to."

"is this what this therapy is about, blaming others? all right james, what was so bad? you seem so angry and so compelled to blame me, i just don't understand it."

"what was so bad? are you kidding me? jesus christ you are completely out of your mind."

"go ahead tell me what was so bad, now's your chance i'm listening."

"i don't know, mom, do you think it's normal for a seven year old to have to come home to an empty house and make himself dinner? god damn spaghetti or a salisbury steak t.v. dinner or stupid boil in a bag macaroni and cheese. what ya think?"

"i don't think you were that young when i started working again."

"i was in first grade, i wasn't even tall enough to see over the damn stove, i had to stand on a chair."

"your father was always home by dinner time."

"bullshit, i never knew when anyone was coming home or what the hell was going to happen when they did, dad on his ass drunk and screaming by six and you'd be home long enough to stir up a bunch of shit and be off again for god knows what and with who."

"i don't know what you're trying to say, james, but don't ever accuse me of being unfaithful to your father, i won't have it, not with him in the cellar right now."

"it's okay mom, i don't think he heard me and anyway let's face it, the only man you were ever faithful to was god."

"i stayed married to your father for forty two years, james david, that's certainly longer than any of the women that have come and gone out of your life. you'd be lucky to find a woman like me."

"believe me i probably haven't found anyone but you."

"well maybe you better start asking yourself why these relationships aren't working out."

"look around."

"well if the worst thing that happened to you is you had a working mother who was a poor cook i think you should be okay."

"you fucking abandoned me! you... bitch and you left me alone or worse you left me with him. if things at home were so bad that you couldn't be here, if you had to spend your entire marriage hiding at church and twenty years in alanon, why do you think it was any better for me?"

i'm furious and crying and trying not to cry like some kid on the playground, blubbering and taking swings and wiping the red snot from his bloody nose on his sleeve.

"i'm sorry you feel that way."
"think about what kind of childhood you had, mom. you hated your mother, you told me that."
"believe me, james, your childhood was very different than mine."
"i doubt it, we just repeat what we know."
"my mother beat me."
"yeah and your father was a drunk like mine."

it's what binds us, the three of us, and ties us to each other and to them. these men, our fathers, the world and the world that broke them. it's their pain we inherit, it's their pasts we can't beat. the old man's past is my beginning as his father's was to him. it's why we're broken and the women around us, me repeating the insanity of this house and him over and over again, screaming and breaking plates and taking swings at the wall. it's a sort of faith, always knowing how things will end.

"well i never laid a hand on you."

"how could you, you were never home."

"i wasn't gone all the time."

"you were at saint joseph's every night, choir, the ladies group, you read to those retarded boys... you gave your time to everyone but me."

"maybe you're right, james, maybe i couldn't face things here, but that doesn't mean i didn't love you."

i've broken her, the pearl of her, the milky film she can filter the world thru. i've busted her but good this time, like the old man's leg, but i can't twist her back into shape. she's crying, smally, shuffling towards the hall, saying her rosary with wordless lips, passing the black beads thru her trite hands, the crucifix end in her robe pocket. i can't see it, but i know it's there like you know the end before it happens. she seems to see something i don't see, something in her sightless eye that i could never see, staring up at the jesus on the yellowed kitchen wall. i find myself looking too, looking up like the faithful do, but i'm as blind as her bad eye. i envy her her faith. maybe it's better in her flick and fitter, in the old fold of her fancy, her whim-wham and titter, all this praying like a motor running until it's its own chaos. what does reality really have for her, but heartache, but an alcoholic husband who did himself in, an only son who can only spit and pity her and never love her. i wished i'd left her to her dreams, but then, even this will have never happened. she'll forget or pretend to, like she pretends to like black toast after she's burnt it. her darling ben at peace finally, her son james is home, isn't that sweet of him. nothing can change in this house, everything will be fine, have faith, offer it up, god is good, go with god, god loves you, god bless. it's what she tells herself like her novenas, day after day, bead after bead, heartache after heartache. it's all she knows.

15

men rage and women sadden like apples on trees, we do what our fathers did, men with hands bigger than ours, boys raised up in this part of the country. but all this water here runs the same way, the trap of a great lake history, granite and gravity. it is written in me, the old man and the whole damn story, everything that haunts me now like the pains of the radiator in the old city apartment, the heat coming on at five and turning off at eight the next morning. the nights are like that, my dime dreams, my small pocket memories.

i peel another slice of ham away, a piece towards the middle and close to the bone, shoving it into my mouth as if it were the last piece. i look for a clean dish towel and wipe my hands on the once white curtains above the sink instead. the fabric yellowed now from suns and hamburger grease and barely holding on like an old tooth. i feel on the edge of something steep, unsteady in my chair, on my feet. i walk over to the phone, my steps are only possible, even doubtful, and death sentence slow and surely coming to an end like everything else. the rain is steady and brutal in its monotony and ultimately futile to be anything, but the lake. i can almost feel the river rising like the threat of a strange man. there is water all around me like i'm drowning, like i'm not even born. water down the windows and up the gravel road. it is our way of life here and eventually the death of us.

"nik?"

"james?"

"yeah it's me, i know it's early, but..."

"i was sleeping, the sun's not even up yet."

"i need to talk to you, i couldn't wait any longer."

"it's not even five yet, what's wrong?"

"jesus christ! what's wrong? i don't know, my father's dead, i'm trapped in this house with my fucking crazy mother, there's no electricity, you and i have split. i guess other than that everything's fine."

"did you call me just so you could scream at me? if so i'm hanging up."

"i'm not screaming, fuck nik, my whole life is falling apart."

"you'll be okay."

"who says? sometimes things aren't okay, i had to live

with that crap thru my whole childhood and it wasn't okay. maybe i won't be okay, maybe some people are just broken."

"the past is just that, james, past, it doesn't matter, all that matters is right now. it's the only thing that's real."

"fuck it, you're right, none of it matters anyway, the fucking river's gone over its banks and it's still raining, there'll be nothing left when it's done, we'll all just wash away, so fuck it why should i care."

"the house may wash away, but you're going to have to deal with the people in it, james. the river's not going to wash that away."

"i don't know, maybe it will wash everything clean."

"you have to deal with how all this is affecting you, you can't live in the past, but you can't just say fuck it, either, it's not that easy."

"nothing's ever been easy for me, believe me, i know that."

"we've all had hardships."

"well i've had a belly full."

"how's your mother? is she happy that you're there?"

"she's got god, she doesn't need anyone else."

"well it's her way of dealing with things."

"it's a fucking crutch, actually it's more like blinders. anyway, i don't want to talk about her. nik i... i want you to move back to the apartment, i want you to be home when i get back. i know we can work things out, mouse, i never stopped loving you."

"well, that's what you want."

"why don't you tell me what you want then, you do the talking for a change."

"we've talked about things."

"you just sit there and look at me."

"you can be very intimidating."

"you can't be pissed off at me for not getting what you want if you can't tell me what you want!"

"it's just gotten to the point where i can't talk to you, not when you're like this."

"like what? what am i doing?"

"i don't feel safe."

"what the fuck does that mean?"

"i don't feel safe when you're acting like you are right now."

"that's such a shit excuse, i'm three thousand miles away, it's not my fault that you're incapable of expressing yourself."

"i have to go."

"go ahead, run away again, run in the bathroom and throw up and tell me you can't talk anymore, that it's all too much."

"james, i can't live with your anger any longer, that's why i left you."

"that's bullshit too, you were gone long before we got into any major argument."

"you've been angry your whole life."

"i'm not angry, i'm just standing up for myself. you're the one that pulled away, you're the one that broke our promise, i didn't do shit."

"i admit, in the past i would've run away, but this time i really tried, i really worked at us, james, i can't take all the drama, i can't do it anymore."

"so was moving out your idea of working on things? my whole issue with you is... is your lack of intimacy and your solution is to put even more space between us and move out. it's all fucking bullshit!"

"listen to yourself, listen to how angry you are, i can't do this anymore..."

there is a muffled sort of silence like she's covered the phone with her hand.

"i can't talk any longer."

"what's going on?"

"james, you need to get help."

"is there someone there with you?"

"james..."

"is there?"

"james, don't do this."

"i guess that means yes."

"i..."

"what the fuck! how the fuck can you do this to me, jesus nik, i don't even know who you are anymore."

"i'm trying to move on with my life."

"we were engaged, you made a commitment. you said you

loved me and then you suddenly decide to move out and never see me again and that's it. fuck! we had a whole life together, how can there be someone else already?"

"i'm a good person, don't try to make me feel guilty. i moved out months ago."

"it's been nine weeks."

"things were over long before i moved out."

"i thought we were working on things with hannalore?"

"james, you're sick. i'm afraid of your temper, breaking chairs and plates, breaking the bathroom door in, it's all i can see when i think of you, i can't be in a relationship with your anger, i can't live like that."

"you hurt me too, you know, it might not be as dramatic, but you did plenty to make me feel like shit about myself. you always looked down on me, even now, i'm the brute, everything's my fault."

"i loved you the best i could."

"i don't know what happened to you, you've become completely heartless."

"i know i made mistakes, but don't say i'm heartless."

"i'll say whatever i want."

"well i don't have to listen."

"you've never once said you're sorry, you think you're little miss perfect with your fucking superior swiss fucking attitude..."

"i'm hanging up now."

"don't hang up on me."

"then don't raise your voice to me."

"yeah, heaven forbid someone show some emotion in this relationship."

"i'm emotional."

"maybe you are, but who'd ever know, you sure as fuck don't show it beyond puking every time we get into a heavy discussion. everything's a fucking secret with you, you're terrified of opening up to anyone, even me and that hurt, it hurt me more than anything, your silence drained me and it drained us."

"so now it's my fault."

"a relationship is all about being intimate and the idea of being intimate scares the shit out of you."

"i don't feel safe with you that doesn't mean i'm afraid of intimacy."

"that's not fair, i wasn't angry about just nothing, anger's a reaction. god, you destroyed me and i fucking let you because i loved you, i loved you more than i loved myself. i could feel you pulling away, i knew i was losing you the second i gave you that fucking ring."

"that's nonsense."

"you didn't even tell your parents or your sister we were engaged. that ripped my heart out."

"they're not like you, james. you wouldn't understand why i couldn't tell them."

"try me."

"i'm not some american girl whose going to run around

giggling and crying and carrying on with her hand out to everyone who comes by about how happy she is, it's no one's business."

"i'm talking about telling your family, nikki. there's a big difference between being demure and being a fucking ice queen."

"i'm not an ice queen."

 "you never loved me."

"that's not true."

"then why the fuck wouldn't you tell your family?"

"because i'd been married before and i was afraid they'd think i was making another mistake."

"jesus, nik."

"now you know, are you happy that you've humiliated me?"

"i'm not humiliating you. how could you have kept that from me?"

"we'd only known each other for a couple of months when you asked me to marry you."

"it was four months, that's a pretty big thing not to tell me."

"i didn't know how to tell you. at first, i didn't think it mattered, then you gave me the ring and i was ashamed to tell you, i didn't know what to say. finally i was afraid to say anything, i didn't know what you'd do."

"you were fucking married!"

"that's why i didn't tell you."

"jesus, are you fucking kidding me, i don't even know

you, that's the saddest thing, we spent two years together and i don't even know you. how the fuck do you live with yourself?"

"it was my private business, you can't tell me i'm a bad person."

"you're a fucking liar, you're sick, you're the one that's sick. i can't take your shit anymore."

"i knew you'd react instead of being understanding."

"i can't understand you if you're a fucking secret to me. all your secret shit killed any chance we had of making it, you never loved me, you can't love anyone."

"don't tell me what i can't do."

"fuck you."

"goodbye james."

"nik, don't hang up on me...nik? ...nik! ...mother fucker!"

i smash the receiver down on the phone, once... and then again, and rip the cord from the wall like the old man always threatened to do. it feels good like a wrong so often does, the pithy ecstasy of a violence. i already know i'm going to destroy it before i do, it's what i do. i throw the phone down on the kitchen floor screaming "fuck" as it explodes into a menagerie of its metal guts, seventies technology and sixties awkward still, transistors and switches made in america, everything in a computer chip now, everything made someplace else, squint and tidy. the linoleum is bruised at the point of impact, the house shut silent again except for the rain and her tip toe feet from somewhere down the hall. her peeking around the corner to see what happened, but never asking, the only question is the sound of my breaths.

nikki was just a girl when i met her, but i pressed her into a diamond, something beautiful and something too hard to love. i could feel it, all of it slipping away, maybe not at my skin, but deep down in some mysterious, purposeless part of my gut, somewhere and something that i thought man had outgrown, an archaic organ like an appendix, something that i can't understand and somehow need to know.

it was new york, it was winter, just after the fall and the fall of our innocence, my innocence and an america. all of us woken from a dream and still rubbing our eyes, the towers gone, people mixing in the ashes with the rain. death seemed everywhere, but she was of the world and used to such things and i was so american and midwest and narrow. i was groggy with the big black sleep of love. i was in love. i was lost in long hair and the soft soft hair of her sex, the whole world where she parted and i was only a part of her. she was everything and everything was central park and peopled with scarves and hats, all their breaths out like ghosts into the air, the skaters there teetering by and shadows everywhere and a sun and sidewalks of pigeons and their pixie feet. we'd gone to new york for christmas, it was the day i lost her.

she was all pretty on a park bench, wrapped like a present and me, i was just beside her like the naked trees and the buildings that were left holding up the sky. i put a ring on her finger, on a knee, a poem and a plea and a pact maybe, if not a promise. and i felt the worn turn of the earth skip and totter like the skaters and a whisper and the infinity of a moment. she was beautiful and i was beautiful because i was part of her and suddenly temporary, true beauty can't last. it is always brief and eventually tragic. it is the circumstance of its death that becomes the very essence of its existence. and maybe all we can pray for is a moment and a memory.

i watched her sleep that night, our first night in new york. we slept with the bathroom light on, otherwise it was too dark to sleep, our window between the buildings and only wide enough for the fire escape. we made love, her eyes kept closed, her hands in the sheets. and she boiled and barely cried out and curled into a little sad slumber after. i laid awake and tried to hold onto what i had already lost knowing i'd already lost the best part of myself as well.

we'd go home new years day, back to the city, our city, to our apartment that was in the sky once and now just on a hill. we played house and happy, but it was over and everything around us. nothing would ever seem the same, only a subtle copy, a paint thin portrait with nothing behind it but a wall.

she loved me i think, but it's hard to know. i know i loved her by the ache in my side still. i don't think i'll ever know why. i don't think i'll ever get that close to god. i barely know what happened and the memories of that certain year or years. in the end i don't know if it even matters if she didn't or did, all that matters is me and what i felt was real, as real as any midnight or jesus. stories never really end or begin, they start with 'and' and end with questions left hanging like old coats in spare bedroom closets. i don't know which lies are true, she was so many things, so many deep welled truths. she loved me i think, but it's hard to know. she was the saddest girl i ever met.

16

our blood lines point to the ground, to the great lake, to a depth we can't know. all this water, like our pasts, pulled up into the center of these storms, rages we raise up from bodies of water, from the north and north-west, dark thoughts that plague us and the region. in our time we will know flood waters and in our lungs again. i'll know, i've always known i'd drown here.

i can't be in the house any longer, not with her all about me like a moth at the porch light, her prayers pecking at the windows, at the doors, his body in the cellar, always beneath me and a symptom of so much more. i can't get nikki out of my head, i'm hollowed out and rattling like a kick to a tin can. i don't know who i am without her, some soul drifting thru our old north beach neighborhood like a fog that comes up broadway, some long forgotten street man sticking out of the sidewalk, remembering something and muttering to himself from his jacket, all rag tatted and elbowed.

where am i, but here again, back home at the begin and alone again, the same only child again. i'm talking to myself like i'm talking to nikki or to him, his rotten body in the cellar, everything ghosts and gone on to inevitable. i can't seem to forget anything, i'm trapped with my memory, with my terminal self, all these thoughts eating away at me until i'm nothing but elements and futile minerals.

she's stooped over in her dime store shadow, picking up pieces of the phone, picking thru the last pieces of nikki and me like she was picking up rice at our wedding. i've got nothing left to say, just sputters and spit.

someday the spell of her will wear off me like paint fading from a fence post or the rusted sign nailed to it that you can only read if you remember what it said. someday she'll be some other girl, the girl i was engaged to once, a ring in the bottom of a drawer, books with the first page torn out that i won't read anymore, but for now she's still too much a part of me to be gone. even the space where she was is something i guess, something more than nothing. she's wedged in me like a splinter that will fester and pulp, something inside of me that i can't pull out, something i'll wear over me like a top coat for years until the next one. then she'll become like the rest of them, a tumor that goes undetected and i'll forget her, but my body will remember her, always. and someday maybe she'll read this and cry.

it's raining still, his slicker in the cellar still, left over from the night before like the puddle of water around his body. she'll wait till i'm at the bottom of the stairs before she speaks, so she can talk into the dark like she talks to her god instead of talking to me.

"is everything okay with you and nicole?"
"well what do you think, mom, i just tore the phone out of the wall and smashed it on the floor. it's probably not a good sign, huh?"
"james, you're such a good man and you work so hard, i just want you to be happy, maybe nicole isn't the right woman for you."
"whatever."
i don't know, i pray for the two of you every day."
"well, it didn't work."
"what did nicole say?"
"it doesn't matter, mom, it's over."
"what happened?"
"a lifetime."
"did nicole say why?"
"i guess it all catches up with you, you're drowning in it

and you don't even know you're in the water."

"well, it's all a part of god's plan."

"i've had enough of god's plan, i've had enough shit for five lifetimes... i don't think nik and i will ever talk again. it's hard to believe, two years together and that's it, a dumb phone call. i don't know, i don't think i know anything anymore."

"prayer has been my salvation, i say a novena for you and nicole every day."

"well you don't have to pray for us anymore."

"it's never too late to pray, james, i say the serenity prayer every morning, it always brings me peace."

"all this god shit, it's all bullshit."

"james david! spirituality is the foundation of our lives."

"you wanna know about god, come on down in this cellar and see what your god made."

"i think i've had enough."

"you're pathetic."

the only sound is the moment after my voice, a kind of silence, the word 'pathetic' remembered in the wood joists and the heating ducts, and then the sounds of her feet on the floor boards towards the kitchen, her irish music playing from somewhere upstairs, her singing just underneath the bauble of the box radio, everything becoming one sound, the sound of my childhood.

everything was quiet then, there were no sounds when he was home, but his sounds, the television and "the booze talking", that's what she'd say, miming me upstairs into my room with my crayons or a book. she'd be out almost every night with choir or the ladies group, any catholic excuse to get out of the house and away from him, away from his breath and his day's beard. the two of us eating t.v. dinners if he ate, otherwise he'd take the foil off for me and drink into the dark until he filled up the room almost to the walls. i'd watch the t.v. with him if there was space, if i was quiet and it wasn't the news, segregation, vietnam, johnson or nixon.

his wrist would say eight o'clock, the oven clock was broken, all it could ever say was three-twenty-two. he'd say it's time for bed from his chair, he'd say good night from the doorway, the smell of whiskey and his oily skin in the air once he left, but not before, only when he shut off my light and walked down the hall, like a stain you don't notice until the wash is done. i thought that's what fathers smelled like, but we can only remember our fathers and never know them. he'd put the light on in their bedroom across the hall so i could see the monsters coming up the steps. so i could hear him downstairs like i could hear the river or the rain storm coming, counting between the lightning and the thunder, counting between the sound of her car on the gravel and his big voice. the two of them fighting downstairs in the kitchen, thru the floor and underneath my bed, and me staying in the crack of light from their room like a slim chance and chewing the end of my blanket.

i put his slicker on again, it's almost habit like it's mine now, but it's borrowed like the rest of me. it still smells of him, i wonder if i smell of him. i wonder if the animals can smell his blood in me, something just under my tongue. i climb back up the stairs knowing i'll have to go down them again. it's raining steady, a good working rain, the kind of rain he liked.

"james are you going out?"
"yeah, i want to check on the near bridge."
"it's raining, do you want to take your father's mercury?"
"no, i need some air, the gravel road's looking a little soft anyway, i don't think you're going to make mass this weekend."
"tim burgermeister is going to pick me up in his monster truck."
"what?"
"tim burgermeister is taking me to mass."
"jesus christ, you're obsessed, have you looked outside? the river is already over the gravel road in spots, i can't imagine what the river road looks like, it's even lower."

"oh it's fine, the gravel road is always a little wet when it's this rainy. tim enters his truck in the county fair every year, he took second prize last year or third."

"you're nuts, what about the bridges, neither one is safe."

"it was second place, i think jenny and will bender's boy was first, i can never remember his name, but tim should have won, it was obvious to everyone there."

"do you even hear me?"

"everything will be fine."

"why's the church thing so important to you that you throw away all common sense, tim fucking whoever in his monster truck, what are you doing? seriously, what is it? isn't your god right here?"

"yes, god is everywhere, that's true, but father ciolek arranged for tim burgermeister to pick me up in his truck and i don't want to disappoint him, they need everyone's help to prepare for easter."

"don't forget your husband's body is in the cellar."

"i lived under your father's thumb for forty two years, james, from now on i'm going to do what i want without all the screaming and yelling."

"well why can't this guy take dad's body to the crematorium or the mortuary or something if he can take you to church?"

"john kapelka is handling your father's body, i'm not going to step on his toes."

"dad's body is in the cellar!"

"james, john will handle everything, he's the mortician."

"so what, dad's fucking body is downstairs and you're going to go to church."

"john kapelka is a professional, there's nothing i can do."

"there's no talking to you, you're fucking crazy, every stupid person in that church is."

"everyone at saint joseph's has been such a support since your father's passing, they always ask about you."

"i don't give a shit."

"why are you so angry?"

"that would take all day."

i leave my mother standing in the kitchen like i'd leave my muddy boots outside. i turn and look back into the living room as i step out the front door, as i absently step into his high rubber boots waiting on the porch boards. my mother in the hall in her old broken dress, she's in tears, her lips are trembling or mouthing a prayer. she's looking at me like she looks at the jesus on the wall, like the day the old man pulled me out of the river.

the first time i died i was just five, i couldn't swim and yet i would play by the river every day. i was playing army or indians or some childhood dally, it was summer, it seemed like july. i was on a rock ledge a few points down from the near bridge, an anonymous spot that would forever after have a name and a faith and become a part of me and a place in my dreams. the rock top was mossy and wet and i was suddenly no longer of the earth, but into the calamity of the air, into the moment of terror before i hit the water and finally the river and the calm of the river's bottom. i remember looking up at the sky as the river pushed me into its palm, into its quiet and its cold. the air was hot and uncertain and something of the past now and everything above me somehow clearer thru the lens of the river than it ever was thru the confusion of the atmosphere.

i wouldn't hear him yelling, but i saw him above me like a big god or a birch tree. he couldn't swim either, but he managed us to shore with forearms he made into roots and some inborn hold to the earth. he told me i was "fucking lucky to be alive" and "god damn it" and his usual parade of profanities and man talk. he pushed on my body til the river came out and the burden of air filled me again. he carried me to the house like you might turn a tourniquet tighter, like some part of him had to die so the rest of him could live. we went straight thru the woods instead of the roundabout way of the gravel road, the sound of leaves and fallen branches under his feet and the sound of his quick breaths mixed with his curse words and nothing else. he pressed my head against his chest with his big hand. his shirt smelled of the river and my wet hair and i closed my eyes and pretended i was in the river still, away from this hoo-hah and his holler, under the water where it was safe.

it's almost all i remember now, like it was the day i was born, like there was nothing before and everything after was only part of that moment. i'm only living now out of habit, momentum maybe, it's nothing i'm trying to do. i'm not afraid of dying, changing maybe, it's this life that is the hard part. i'm always waiting for something, for the water, maybe, for the rain or the river to kill me and wash me clean and carry me into the next life if there is one. i came into this world wet and crying out, out of her and the river the same. now i walk the golden gate every sunday and wonder why i don't just go over the rail, back into the water waiting like it does. i look down at the bay and its choppy mystery and pray for the certainty of those long moments of the river again, of my lungs full of quiet again, like it seemed to belong there, a life and a death again.

the gravel road seems wet from beneath like the rain is coming up out of the ground, like a feeling something is going to happen. the river is everywhere, its banks broken-hearted, but we can't keep love, that's why we love, all our tiny tries at eternity and beautifully vain. the river's pall is at the trees, washing their past summer's leaves away like they never had a past. there is only now and the rain and the river and the last portions of the gravel road that remain above the water, the old house four steps higher, but no higher. i can feel the river's hate from a mile away, the old man would say eight-tenths, stepping thru the lazy water that has collected on the gravel road and the rain with no real place to go. i can hear the river's chest beating like the bass of a freight train, the pull at its center is full and fierce. its current has broken loose like some teenage runaway on a love me not killing spree, whole trees swept up in its dreaming, trash and an old car tire, glimpses of flat boards churning in its sleep. i know there's things dying in the river, but they are invisible and trapped to the bottom and will only be found weeks later. and there are things that will never be found, things washed to the lake and hidden and missed maybe and mourned or not missed and never prayed for. this lake holds onto its dead, some sort of forever if you're looking. its waters saltless and heavy and deeper than the ocean, maybe, and surely more secret. it is the end and by some magic of the air and the sun, the beginning. its rain the life of a wanting earth and the blood sap of the river, but that's the trick of any god i suppose, some life out of death, some mix of elements and eternity.

the river is at the top of the near bridge, the crooked '36 my grandfather drew already forgotten under the cock sure of the water. in the next few hours the river will cover the bridge, if the bridge holds. otherwise, there will be nothing again, only the river and the woods and the ghosts of indians, maybe bones of rebar and a brief recollection of cement and stone where something stood once. the force of the flood is not of this time, but of a beginning of time when the earth was first cut. when everything was of god and mattered. everything will be different when it's done, when the rains stop and the flood waters die into the lake and into the ground and wait for their sovereign's sign to return. even i will be forever changed, my form gouged out from all this water, the same water that cut my path before, a life i had to follow, but rivers don't have choices, only fates.

there is a truck speeding from around the bend on the gravel road just before the near bridge, i can only see it, the sound of the river is everything else. it's an old chevy body above a frightening mesh of purposeful shafts and struts and tires that seem as big as a tractor's. it doesn't hesitate, but motors across the bridge doing forty or forty five. a short blonde, bearded man is behind the wheel, he nods his head instead of waving as he passes by, his hands on the wheel like he's strangling his ex-girlfriend, perhaps he thinks of it as the same. the truck bounces and fish tails slightly and heads down the gravel road sending the flooded sections into the air with a roar under his wheel wells and over the truck's cab. i can't see him, but i can imagine him hooting and pounding his fist on the wheel every time he hits the water like a playground bully would work a puddle.

"jesus christ...what a fucking idiot."

the rain has no answer and the river probably thinks us all fools. i start back towards the house for nothing else to do. i'll tell her why she shouldn't go, but she'll go. she'll say everything will be fine and burgermeister will suck at his teeth like he just ate a tough steak and smile satisfied that he got something with his tongue and they'll drive away. to spite me she will be fine and i'll be here with him and the house again, goddamn alone again waiting for her to come home and for the water.

17

 the house is an accordion of lights and pilot light gas, of the radio and clutter, of muddy carpets and burnt wax. she's buzzing above like a numb worker bee, busy hands at her hat and her hair and painting nail polish on a pair of pantyhose with another run. i know her, her tit for tat, her whim wack, her cake batter make-up to fill in the cracks and cheap jewelry, clip on earrings and always everything too much like old women do.

"tim, help yourself to the ham and there's jello if you want, james hates it, so eat as much as you want."

she's screaming down the stairs, she's probably in the bathroom smiling in the mirror, putting on her lipstick and her drug store perfume that will fill the house for the rest of the day. there's barely enough air left for her irish music blaring from the speaker box radio in the downstairs bedroom, it is only between her desperate powders and creams. everything is about her and about her and around us like old spider webs across the stairs down into the cellar.

burgermeister looks up from the ham he's putting into his mouth as i walk into the kitchen. he looks at me with a kind of awe saved for mass murderers or amputees. i can only stare back at him and wonder if i bite. he's eating my food, i have an urge to kill him, an impulse i barely notice from somewhere in the old part of my brain, some last bit of instinct i haven't lost yet, like a stab of love or jealousy. he's a small man, but something you couldn't break or break into something smaller, the lowest denominator of common. he's thirty or thirty five, he smells of cigarettes and the smell a winter coat develops by spring. he's wearing a red flannel shirt and levi's and square toed frye boots like he should, though, there is an uncertainty around him like you can never quite hear him or see him.

"you don't like jello, god, man i love jello."
"it's a little runny, it's been out since yesterday."
"it's cool man."
"it's really been raining, you think the road's safe?"
"aw, shit yeah, that chevy, she's a good girl, she'll go anywhere, ya know she took third place last year at the county fair."

"yeah, i heard, congratulations."

"thanks man, it was tough competition, but i'm gonna win this year, i just put a new chip in her, extra thirty horses."

"that's great. good luck."

"thanks, but it ain't no luck, it's pure skill, it's no different than the indy five hundred or daytona, just the best man and machine."

"what about the bridges, i know the bridge up here on the gravel road is really getting rocked, i can't imagine what's going on with the wood bridge down close to town."

"well the way i figure it is you take 'em at full speed, see, then you ain't weighing down on the bridge as much."

"well actually your speed isn't going to change your weight."

"whata ya talking about, man, how do you think airplanes take off the ground, hell i figured you to be smart, living in california and all, book smart i guess, your mom says you're some sort of artist or somethin', can't teach ya common sense, though, ya either got it or you don't."

"well i don't know about that, but..."

"don't worry, man, i know these roads and all like the back of my hand, i've lived here all thirty one years of my whole life."

"i grew up here too and i saw a lot of floods, but i never saw the river like this, not this high, it's over the flood mark of thirty six."

"that's what i mean, common sense will tell ya if the

bridge's held up this far that it ain't goin' nowhere."

"how's the jello?"

"i told ya, i love jello, there's no such thing, but good jello."

"you have breakfast this morning?"

"yep, had me steak and eggs at carolanne's place first thing, splurgin' on myself a bit, made more money since these rains started than i did the first four months of the year plowin' snow, best thing that ever happened."

"how's that?"

"see i got a business mind, it's common sense, man. if ya don't have a boat, the only way into town is in that truck out there and the road is way safer than the river."

"how much are you charging?"

"fifty cash for a ride into town."

"really?"

"yep, and folks will pay it, i been runnin' without a break since yesterday."

"that's great, well like my mom said, eat up, i'll go see what she's doing."

i leave him at the kitchen table, he's eating the jello out of the pyrex pan it was made in, he's holding his spoon like a shovel, his chin to the edge of the pan so he can scoop it right into his mouth. again i have the urge to kill him, but this time it's purely conscious and only out of disgust.

"what a fucking idiot."

he won't hear me, the volume of the music is on the edge of mania and the middle of distortion. it circles around me until i think i might fall. i start up the stairs, the sound of bag pipes and gay fiddles follow me, her perfume already half way down the stairway. she's in the bathroom, the bathroom door is open, she's singing some nonesense to the radio or to herself as if she knew the words.

"james isn't it wonderful, the electricity is back on and tim's here to take me to saint joseph's, it's the power of prayer."
"are you paying this idiot a hundred dollars to take you to church?"
"i'll be back sometime around six, maybe you could go thru your father's things while i'm gone and set aside what you want."
"will you answer me please."
"i think i can make my own decisions about whether i go to church or not."
"well dad would be spinning in his grave if he knew you were spending a hundred dollars to get to town and back, that is if he were in a grave and not in the goddamn cellar."
"i have my own life now and i'm going to do what i want for a change without all the hubbub. i just want peace. please james, just let me be."
"you're crazy."
"and i am not going to bury your father, uhhh, the thought

of him being buried in the ground... i could never do it, i'm very claustrophobic."

"well it's not about you, it's about dad and i don't think dad wanted to be cremated."

"your father told me to do what was easiest for me and cremation is what is easiest for me, he's my husband and i'll do what i want with his mortal remains."

"well it's not very catholic."

"james, your father hadn't been to mass in thirty years. in all the years we were married he never heard me sing. and now he never will. father ciolek has been very understanding, i already talked the whole thing over with him, he's been very supportive."

"well at least you talked it over with him, you sure as hell didn't talk it over with me. if i hadn't caught up with the hearse i would've never seen him again."

"i know you loved your father, james, but you have to let go, ashes to ashes, that's what the bible says."

"it's impossible to talk to you, i give up."

"what's that? dear."

"you have no idea what i'm talking about, ever! i haven't been home in twelve years, your husband's body is in the basement and you're going off to church. let me tell you, nothing's changed around here, you just go about like it's just another day, fuck it, go ahead, go take care of your friends."

"do you want me to stay, if you want me to stay here at the house i will. i'll tell tim you don't want me to go."

"i don't want you here, i don't want anything from you."

"okay, then i'll see you at a little after six... oh and go look thru your father's things so we don't throw anything out that you'd want, i'm starting monday right after the memorial. you wait and see what this place is going to look like, i'm going to clean everything out and fix the holes in the roof and the porch and... well you'll see it's going to be a brand new house."

"and where's the money coming for all this?"

"your father left me very well taken care of don't worry."

"i will worry, what are you going to live on?"

"your father has money hidden all over the house, there's probably ten thousand in the chest freezer alone, you know the way he was, he only put enough money in the bank to cover the electric bill, he never trusted tim kucinich."

"who?"

"tim kucinich down at the bank, your father said he was suspended from junior high for going thru lockers at lunchtime. they all went to school together."

"well you've never paid a bill in your life, you have no understanding of money even if you have it."

"i did all of alanon's bills for almost two years until laurie ann rowen took them over, i was fine doing them, but laurie's father had died and she couldn't afford the house on her own and needed ... well i can't talk about this now, tim's waiting downstairs."

"thank god."

she'll be gone and a sort of silence will settle into the plaster and the peeling paint from the ceiling and a sound beneath the quiet, a hum i can only hear with the thick of my legs and arms and the bones in my back. i've wandered into my old room, i've got nowhere to go, i'm looking out the small bedroom window at the rain gathering on the gravel road. this is the end, i am convinced of that. everything is easy, thoughtless, our consequence decided and only to be lived out.

i'll wait till they drive away before i go thru his things, his closet shelf and his top dresser drawer, places that were too high and too hushed to ever dare when i was really young. i need to be alone when i do, i don't know why, like saying his secrets out loud is okay if there's no one to hear them. he kept his cash money there, his old papers in the drawer, heavy pens and mechanical pencils, tie tacks he didn't wear anymore and pins and kennedy half dollars and rubber bands and stamps and a good wood smell, the pungence of a postaged, noticed, licensed past. when i was old enough to, i'd steal a five or even a ten sometimes for the movies and gas and road beers and screw top wine. i'd look at the pieces of his life all together like the alluvium at the end of the river, what he brought home in sample jars and on the bottom of his boots and over his pant legs, and wonder what happened to his time.

maybe i'll put his cuff links in my pockets, slip his school ring on, stick his national honor society pin in my collar. maybe i'll jump in the river, find myself at the bottom again, they'll have their own reasons when they find me. and maybe they'll never find me and i'll become part of the lake and a myth, a line in her savage faith and something they never knew or suspected.

she's shouting up the stairs, over the music, it's what we always did, no one ever talked to anyone in this house. we only hollered and howled, bawled talk between walls, down the stairs or up the hall, over the radio or the t.v., the old man screaming shut up.

"james, we're leaving, do you want me to leave the radio on for you?"
"no!"
"okay, enjoy, enjoy."
"i don't want it on."
"what? darling."
"the hell with it ... nothing!"
"i should be back around six!"
"fine!"
"look thru your father's things, there's some pretty neat stuff!"

"whatever mom."

"what?"

"fine! just go, i'll see you later."

"bye! love you!"

i let her "love you" hang in the air and die on the window sill like a winter fly. she waited by the door for me to say "love you too..." and told herself i didn't hear her. she'll tell burgermeister that it's so hard to hear anything from up the stairs, that the house was designed that way with the bedrooms in mind and think out loud how great a son i am and how special our relationship is and how much i loved my father and how much my father loved me and not really know a thing about either one of us.

i listen for the sound of his truck starting and the gravel under the tires, if not the water, before i start into their room. i stop at the door like it's the door to a church or a strip club, someplace that requires an extra breath, a held breath, before you enter.

"jesus, not a fucking thing's changed in here."

i whisper because of the silence, because i'm supposed to, because some places you must. there is a supernatural quiet regardless of the radio's racket below, "her music" a ghost thru my head, too much of my memory and nothing real to me now. an absurd irish dirge drifting up the

stairs and thru their room into the sour light there, the
dour smell of old clothes in the closet, callouses and lost
hair. the lamp on her night stand is lit, but hopeless. his
nightstand is piled with newspapers and dirty clothes and a
clock radio blinking 12:00 12:00 12:00 in a chemical way,
its red light acid in the air. his dresser is where it always
was, the only place it could be, four rows of secrets and
socks, t-shirts and underwear. i open the top drawer with
the same ceremony as kapelka pulling the sheet back from
the old man's dead face. every moment now seems slowed
down and important, some sort of morality play with a
lesson i've yet to learn. everything inside is the same as
i remember, odds and ends, paper clips and bank pens.

there is an old wallet, worn brown and bent with his seat.
i fold it open like a day flower, it is filled with an inch of
twenties and yellowed school pictures of me, one from
each year until we'd both quit caring. there are four slit's
for credit cards and such behind a scratched clear plastic
cover and a lean faced drivers license poking out that
expired in seventy-three, a cloverleaf bowling alley pass
good for 1971 behind it. and there is a lock of hair, the
color of mine or his, some iconic bit of voodoo, wedged in
with a picture of me with a twelve pound pike according
to the back of the photo. i was ten. the old man caught it,
but he gave me the rod and let me pull it into the net that
stretched out from his arm. i sat quieted and smalled at

the front of the boat staring into its mouth like it was the good eye of god. it was a magnificent thing, scaled and horrible and beautiful all at once, teeth and the mystery of deep water and most likely older than the earth.

below his wallet is the leather looking plastic box he kept his wedding ring in. he never wore it, he said rings were dangerous for a man that works with his hands. he told me again and again that my grandfather only had four of his fingers from a farming accident. he neglected to say he'd lost a thumb. i still think of him every morning just before i start to work, his words of warning like a prayer or a fight speech or some dirty joke i can never tell the same way. i open the lid, the box lid snaps open almost on its own. the interior is red velvet and strewn with cuff links and tie tacks and all the shinies i remember as a kid, a watch band and a stamp from italy and his selective service card, june 5, 1954, signed by him and a registrar named bernice carlson. i follow my finger over his signature, i don't know why, but it seems i have to as if it were some test to see who i am. next to the box is a stack of small sample envelopes the size of silver dollars, they are scribbled with dates, 3-7-68, 5-16-68, 8-1-68, 1-19-69 and such, inside are bits of bloody white baby teeth, my teeth. it's strange to think about them here at home in his dresser drawer and the rest of me someplace else. i wonder where nikki is right now and what became of my grandfather's thumb.

i want to put my teeth back in my mouth where maybe
they can root and i can put myself back together again.
looking at them makes me sad, not even sentimental, but
quietly heartbroken like a saint who knows enough to be
quiet and heartbroken. i stuff the little envelopes of teeth
down deep into my jeans pockets, another piece of me
that's fallen off, some bit part in this slow erosion.

under the envelopes are newspaper articles carefully cut
and folded like handkerchiefs, little ridiculous snips of
newsprint, "tully scores 23 in title victory over bears" and
"redmen win their 10th straight" and later reviews from the
chronicle and the herald, "north beach artist's opening..."
"new sculptor...interesting", "derivative", "fresh vision",
"postindustrial commercialization".

"what the fuck do they know anyhow. i bet none of them
ever scored 23 points in a conference title game."

i laugh out loud, it sounds strange coming out of me and
brutal and nothing funny, but the symptom of a malady,
maybe a madness or an abandon of hope, the neighbor's
dog you've known for years suddenly baring its teeth. i
grab a shoe box from the closet and dump the brown
crooked shoes that were left there onto the closet floor. i
carefully begin emptying his drawer into the box, mim-
icking the arrangement as if it were an archeological dig

and then another box and another until there are four
boxes and the drawer is empty except for odd insurance
company pens and rubber bands and loose pennies and a
rubber change holder that says first national bank, paper
clips and a fingernail clipper with a fish on the lever and
a silver baby spoon from the niagara falls gift shop on the
canadian side which made it exotic. it was the farthest
away he ever went, they went for their honeymoon, two
days in buffalo.

the closet is filled with nothing but shit, they always are,
everything you don't want to see and think you'll need
someday. "a perfectly good" suit coat with six inch lapels,
another suit coat freshman slim and moth eaten, ties equal-
ly wide or thin and worn out like a good idea that just
didn't work. everything is at their ends, early fifties to late
seventies, times when men still wore suits. he'd wear them
when he went east on the river road and to the highway,
to the city and the city college there or to his big meetings
with the state people about the lake. i never knew what he
did, but he went almost every other week, showered and
shaved and uncomfortable, smelling of menthol shaving
cream and rubbing alcohol. he never went to the university, but that was straight south on the highway and away
from the rivers and two hours from the lake. he'd send
them samples every week though like you'd send someone
a postcard of someplace they'd never been, but read about.

i don't know if any of those students there ever stood in the river or watched the color of the lake change. i'm not sure what they knew, trying to see an apple studying a jar of apple sauce.

i know every jacket hanging in his closet, familiar faces without names, but places, what i can still see behind him, his baby blue or brown or plaid arm out the window, waving goodbye as i chased his truck thru the woods to the near bridge or sundays when i was young and he still went to church and pretended to pray. below his suit coats and shirts and pants and sometimes a vest are his good shoes that aren't so good anymore, an old man's shoes, cracked and unpolished and almost worn thru. there are two bowling bags back behind everything else, below the clothes hanging on hangers. only one has a ball in it, his ball, a solid black brunswick, fourteen pounds and drilled with three finger holes large enough to be thumbs. i stretch my hand and my fingers in, but i can barely reach. his hands were tremendous, often frightening and something of a time gone by when men possessed such things. they hung from his arms like separate creatures, too powerful to be owned or a part of anything but themselves and able yet to prepare sample slides with the delicacy of a wet nurse. my hands are working hands, roughened with day shifts and evenings at the studio, what looks more like a tool shop, what was an old garage when i bought it. my hands are the story of my life, lined and calloused and crooked fingered and scarred to remember, probably extraordinary and seemingly common because they're mine.

i look down at all he's dragged along till now, his moraine on the floor, his life in four shoe boxes like the fleeting samples he took from the river, just facts and nothing more. i'll carry them downstairs, one stacked on top of another, down the hall past the cellar steps to the kitchen. i know what to do now, i suppose some part of me always knew, old bread bags and duct tape. it'll all make sense someday if it doesn't make sense now.

18

the night has filled in the room like a man's voice, like a woman's name, something spoken when it should be sang, something black and not black, but almost blue and from deep in the earth, from the bottom of the lake and leached into an already dark sky. the rain has stopped, the crickets starting, their hysteria in the air or in my head and forever some part of my inheritance until i've nothing else. i've just come awake. i don't know where i am, a wall clock tapping its fingers, memorizing each step of my death. i'm in the living room, i think, or in the long sleeve of a bad dream. i've been sleeping on the couch, i don't remember lying down. everything is in a dusk church light, the only light from six seven day candles, three saints still burning, two madonnas and a jesus. the smell of candle wax i won't forget, it will always be the smell of his death. it was the smell of sex once and suppers in the apartment on jones, of her and her soft revenge. now it is the smell of the end, our end and his. it seems everything is gone. everything i stood on has disappeared and left me doubting the earth, if not myself, like i'll look down and not see my feet.

the space where his chair was seems sadder than his old rind in the cellar, the side table still there, newspapers and a t.v. guide, the four boxes i filled with his drawer stacked on the coffee table in front of me, each wrapped in a bread bag and covered in layers of duct tape. i've been sleeping on my arm, my hand all pins and needles, its imprint pressed red into my face. it's after seven, she's late, she was always late. maybe she won't come home this time, maybe the wood bridge gave into the river finally, maybe she's passed on like the old man, forever in the palm of her god's hand. maybe she's dead like i always thought, always waiting for her after school an hour and a half past when she said she'd be home, waiting and eating cereal out of the box and watching batman and superman and gilligan's island if the antenna was right.

and him, he's here, down in the cellar, under a sheet like his mother's old wickerwork chairs in the attic. i shake the flashlight to life and open the cellar door, stepping down into the dark with an abruptness as if i was jumping in cold water, a violence of momentum so i won't stop or stop to think and thinking how the electric is back on and reaching back and flipping the light switch with my elbow, my hand on the flashlight still. i fall into the cellar like i'm falling in the deep part of the river, into a current i can't help and the weak light of the thirty watt bulb above me, the old man too cheap to use sixty watt bulbs or even forty fives. the house was always dim like everything was in the shadow of something, something that was too big to see, some secret we'd held for so long we'd forgotten what it was. the steps groan and threaten to quit. there's an inch of water across the floor, just below the hissing pilot of the furnace and the water heater. his body is under the work light like he's working again and drinking like always and finally passing out like he did. the fluorescent tubes buzzing above him, giving off a sure element of light and an inkling of another life.

"james, i'm home. james, are you here? jaaaaaames?"
"i'm in the cellar!"
"i have wonderful news, i saw john kapelka at mass, he told me he's coming to get your father tonight so they can cremate his remains and have them back first thing monday morning... with god's grace we should have your father's ashes by ten for the memorial."
"what?"
"i saw john kapelka at mass, he's made all the arrange- ments with the crematorium, they're staying open till he and tim get there tonight."

"you're going to let that fucking idiot with the truck take dad's body?"

"i thought that's what you wanted."

"do you trust this guy?"

"james, tim is a perfectly fine young man, he's at church every sunday, you went to school with his brother."

"so what if i went to school with his brother, they could both be serial murderers for all i know."

"oh, such nonsense, john kapelka will be overseeing every-thing anyway, everything will be fine, father blessed tim's truck today when mass was over."

"what?"

"father ciolek blessed 'sweetheart' before tim brought me back, your father will be fine."

"who the hell is sweetheart?"

"oh that's what we call the truck."

"that's what 'we' call the truck. you can't be my mother, i must have been mixed up at birth."

"oh don't be so silly."

"where are they going to put his body?"

"in the back, tim's borrowing bob radzinski's cap thing-amajig, you know, oh it's all so technical, but, well your father will stay dry, although the rain has stopped. i don't think it's going to rain anymore tonight and it never rains on easter sunday."

"where do you come up with this shit? of course it rains on easter sunday."

"i'm going to be sixty two years old this july twelfth and

i've lived my entire life here, well except for my years at hunter, but otherwise i've lived my whole life here and i don't remember a single easter when it rained, really, not a one."

"i don't doubt that, you definitely have your own catholic memory of things."

"james, you're so bad... have you gone thru your father's things?"

"i have a few more things to do down here so don't let anyone down till i'm done. the cellar's flooding, it's a big mess down here."

"your father kept everything important up off the floor, that cellar is always wet, you can smell it from upstairs."

"well whatever, just give me some time."

"tim's headed off to john kapelka's house right now. he's bringing john back here. try to hurry, james, they're going to want to get going, it's easter tomorrow and the crematorium is staying open tonight especially for your father. your father was very well respected. we're so blessed."

"are you kidding me, blessed? i think cursed might be a better word."

"god has his own way, james, i just know that everything always works out in the end."

"what makes you think things always work out?"

"because i have my faith."

"...i envy you that."

neither of us knows what to say. i'm looking up the stairs to where her voice was and at the single bulb above the steps like it's the light of a mishap star, the old man's body left behind me like some weekend project. everything is seemingly behind me and below the earth to where the water starts. everything is only water now and as elusive as a rain. i'm crying, i don't know when it started, i'm afraid i might never stop. i walk up the cellar stairs leaving a wet boot mark on each step, a sort of forgiveness if not a regret. i'm sobbing, heaving tears so i can barely climb the steps. i climb the steps and retch, water pouring out of me, tears and snot, every last bit wrung out of me and hung on the line, only the wind and time to do the rest. i can barely speak, but my voice comes out of me, who i've always been.

"mom, i don't know what to believe anymore..."
"james?"
"dad and nikki, they're gone, they're just memories and i'm afraid i won't remember enough and they'll disappear or even worse i won't be able to forget and it will drive me crazy..."
"time heals."
"it's all just so much so fast, i don't know what to do, i'm afraid i'm not going to make it."
"james, i know you're hurting, god doesn't hand us

anymore than we can hold, i keep telling myself that and saying the serenity prayer whenever i feel down, pray, god will answer."

"i don't think i believe in god anymore, i don't know what i believe."

"i'd rather believe in god and be wrong than not believe and be right."

"mom, i'm so sad, i'm ..."

"i know james, i know you loved your father and i know you love me. no matter what you say, i know that. and i know how much you loved nikki, you were good to her, i watched you, everybody makes mistakes."

"she cut me so deep, i feel like the bleeding won't ever stop. you hurt me, i know you didn't mean to, but you hurt me too, i was a little kid, you were all i had."

"i love you, james, you know that, you're my only child, i wanted to give you a brother or a sister, god knows i tried, i had six miscarriages after i had you, i still think it was that damn river, all those chemicals your father was exposed to, anyway, the last one almost killed me, do you remember the last time, when you were ten and i was pregnant and i had to go to the hospital?"

"i found you."

"i thought your father came home and found me."

"i found you. dad was at the river, i called the sheriff."

"oh, it's funny how you remember things, the doctor said i was dead when the paramedics got there, but i remember everyone standing over me like i was already in a grave, your father and that young deputy sheriff and then the men from the ambulance and my mother was sitting in that old green chair that we've kept all these years, that's what i remember, she'd been dead for years of course, but i could see her just sitting there watching me like she would watch a loaf of bread baking, you loved that chair, you played king arthur sitting in it with that aluminum foil crown you made at school. anyway, everyone was circled around me, above me looking down and they were breathing all my air so there was none left, sucked it right out of me, i swear. james, promise me you won't bury me, i can't stand it, i want to be cremated, the thought of being buried, ughh..."

"mom, please let's take care of dad, i can't talk about all this stuff right now, you're all i have left."

"you'll always have god."

"i need something i can hold onto, i need something real, something that doesn't fall thru my hands. why can't you understand that? all i've ever had is promises, i've been waiting my whole life for some fairytale, for everything to be okay, it's not okay, it's not going to be. i'm forty and i've got nothing, just a bunch of broken promises. what am i waiting for? for you? for dad? for nikki?"

"all i know is to put your trust in god, james, in the end it's all we have."

"mom, please don't cremate dad, please, i need to know

where he is, when you're gone, my whole life is gone, i'll have nothing."

"james, that's not your father down in the cellar, you said so yourself, your father has gone into god's hands now."

"i could always count on him, even if he was drunk, in his own way he was there for me."

"you were the apple of his eye, he talked about you every day, james. he didn't come out to see you because he was ashamed, he didn't want you to see what he'd become, he knew better than anyone that he was an alcoholic."

"i wish he could have seen what i did."

"your father was a brilliant man, he unfortunately never believed in himself, but he believed in you. he has every review ever written about you and your sculptures."

"he never saw any of them, it kills me that he never saw them, that he never will, that was it, he's done."

"he has the pictures you sent, every piece, the polaroids, they're in the glove compartment in your father's car, he showed them to everyone in town, probably to everyone he ever met. he was so proud of you, james."

"i feel like i don't even know who he was."

"you're just like him, when he was young when i first met him, before all the alcohol, you just have to look at yourself."

"i don't want to be like him or live his life."

"you won't, you moved to california to have your own life."

"but i'm not, i've inherited his... i don't even know what...

his pain, this self hate, a sort of darkness. i'm drawn to it like some sort of goddamn perverse moth, every woman i've been with has been broken. they all have some secrets eating away at them from the inside out, they've all been some version of him."

"isn't this anna laura helping you with all that?"

"it's hannalore, and yes, she's trying. it's hard."

"you've never been a drinker."

"no, not really."

"believe me james, you're not living your father's life. he wouldn't have wanted you to. your father killed himself, i watched him every day."

"it's not that simple, the booze was just a way to dull things down, it wasn't the problem, it was something else."

"i know your childhood wasn't what you wanted it to be."

"mom, my childhood was a train wreck."

"we all suffered."

"what happened to him?"

"your father's childhood was very difficult, your aunt veronica told me about her and your father when they were kids a few months before she died. dear god, it will be four years come christmas time. jesus, mary and joseph. you remember she had that terrible cancer."

"yeah."

"your father brought her soup every week. veronica practically raised your father, both your aunts and your uncle were much older than him, veronica was the next youngest

and she was ten years older than your father. your grandparents had nothing to really do with him, your grandpa
tully worked at the ohio drive shaft, he'd drive into the city
on monday and come back fridays, he slept in the car for
years. your grandmother took care of the farm with your
uncle and your aunts, your father was too young to do any
heavy chores so he sat in the house by himself. vernie, they
called her vernie, she took care of him at night starting
when he was just a baby, she was more a mother to him
than anyone. i think that's why he loved the river so much,
vernie said they'd come in from the fields and find him
there, up on that rock down from the near bridge, always
reading, studying things, building things with sticks and
rocks he'd found, your father lived in his mind, like you,
he was a thinker."

"didn't he ever talk about his childhood with you?"

"no, he never spoke of it, ever, you know how quiet your
father was, frank stuckley was your father's only friend
when he was young, they've known each other since they
were six. he told me your father didn't even talk in school
until he was a teenager."

"i want dad's old river clothes."

"oh you can't wear them, they're horrible, i mean to throw
them out, i can't even give them away they're so stained
with that damn river and those filthy samples he pulled."

"i want to dress dad in them, i don't want him riding in

the back of that idiot's truck in a hospital gown. i know
his work clothes are what he's most comfortable in."
"james, john kapelka is handling ..."
"mom, please just do this for me, okay, then you can cremate him, you can do whatever you want."

she's looking at me like the madonna on the candle, a
sort of sorrow one only knows after it's too late. but she
doesn't know, she never will. i know and i will live with it
and with him always inside me and the knowing at least
where a part of me will end.

19

his old work clothes are more of the river now than of him and really of the earth, what the river carries and never the water itself. the river only passes by us, maybe thru us, eternally temporary, a moment and a momentum. but there is water always around us, the lake and the rain and a neverness, a circle we can't trace and unwittingly follow. she is collecting his clothes, his flannel shirt frayed at the cuffs and collar, his duck canvas pants too tough to wear, only soften, his muck boots on the front porch where i left them, a graying v-neck undershirt in the second drawer. i follow her thru the house like an altar boy repeating a ritual i don't know, something i can only understand while it's being done and never after.

"they're not clean, i should wash them."
"mom, just leave 'em."

"they're so dirty though, your father was working the day he died. he was still at the river when i came home from saint joseph's. he was walking up the gravel road, he'd been driving lately because of the chest pains, but he was walking, i think he sort of knew it was the last day. i yelled out from the kitchen porch that he was starting to walk like an old man, he smiled, he was embarrassed to open his mouth anymore, you know he didn't have any of his teeth left, all the sugar in the booze i'm sure... anyway, he smiled with his lips together and he gave me the finger and he looked at me again like it was the first time he saw me."

"mom?"

"it's all right, i'm okay... your father brought those daffodils over on the kitchen window, your grandma tully planted them everywhere, she sold them palm sundays and easter. your father had them with him in his sample box, they're my favorite, well except for daisies of course, they're my absolute favorite and queen anne's lace, your father always said they were weeds, but i love them. anyway, your grandma tully, god rest her soul, she'd take those eggs to town every day except sundays and daffodils in spring. paul klusky, he must be close to ninety three or ninety four, he remembers, he always says to me 'we always knew it was spring when mrs. tully came around with the flowers' that's what he says every time i see him at church around this time of year."

"mom, where are dad's catfish gloves? i can't find them."

"oh, i threw those out first thing, the stench from those gloves are enough to chase the holy spirit away, catfish biopsies were one of your father's big things. he always said there was no better way to tell what was in the lake than by what was in a catfish, horrible things they are and mean, those stingers, ughh."

"are they in the trash heap?"

"james, you don't want them they're just awful."

"i need them."

"you can't wear them, james, you'll never get the stench out of them.

"mom, i just need them, okay."

"well i can't imagine what you'd want with those disgusting gloves, but they're in the ash pile if you want them, they're buried in a couple of days trash, but i guess they can't get any worse. i had to throw everything in the freezer out, thank god your father isn't here, it would have killed him to see all that food go to waste, especially the pierogies."

"what?"

"he made the pierogies for saint joseph's easter feast, he must have made two hundred this year, i had to throw all of them out."

"dad made pierogies for the church?"

"you wouldn't believe it, they're always the most popular thing at the buffet, he'd never go, twenty years or more now, everyone would say 'tell ben we loved the pierogies', it was his mothers recipe, she made them for the feast for years, until she passed on, god rest her soul."

i'm already moving thru the kitchen, pushing the back
screen door open, it's bottom corner scraping fresh wood
into the porch boards. the remaining hinge will break soon
i'm sure, only magic is holding it now, no metal or math
makes sense. the door will never be fixed, it will fall and
be put against the side of the house where it will sit for
years until she's dead. its buckled posture seems to mean
something, something that makes me hesitate and squint
with thought and almost dream, but eventually it is only a
broken screen door and i can walk down the steps forgetful
if not forgiven. the flash light is still in my hand, my hand
wet around the pitted steel like anything you hold onto
for too long. my shadow is stretching out from my boots
onto the rock stones, the two floodlights above the porch
door behind me, their nerve at the trees, but not between.
it is only black there and lush with black sounds, secrets
of insects eating at the air and at themselves, the grind of
calcium teeth and collagen scraping at the trash, rotten
meat and potato peels, animals at the ground and last
fall's leaves, their feet into the woods as my scent fills the
air and the path behind the shed house to the trash heap.

it's dark behind the shed house, just the flashlight beam
jerking over a scattered pile of garbage and a ring of chick-
en wire fence, the ruined food thawed from the freezer,
what they ate and didn't eat. the fire pile is to the right,
ashes and rusty cans, bright boxes yet to be burned, cracker boxes and cereal boxes and a swollen box of salisbury

steak. his gloves are next to a spent can of chili and a stack of soaked papers. they're heavy with rain, gray with bands of blue and red stitching like work gloves always are. i reach over the wire and grab them, i put my hand inside, wiggle my fingers, make sure i'm alive. the large cuff up over my forearms, each glove so big they could hold both my hands. i look down at my feet, at myself poking up out of the ground, my shadow stretching back into the trees and the dark they breathe in and quietly out. i'm at the start of his arm, the end of his grip, under his skin. i shudder and slip the gloves off, the flood lights blinding my walk back to the house like i'm some mole crawling thru the grass in the sun.

they'll be here soon, burgermeister and kapelka, i don't have time to mull things over. i work best from my chest anyway, somewhere where i don't have to think, where i can just do, like a blue sunday or a bad morning, some mood that just happens, maybe the residue of a dream, something i know, but i don't know why. there's no purpose in drawing over a straight line, anyhow, or anything but a straight line between two points. i'll do it quick and it'll be done, his clothes hung over the kitchen chair where he sat sitting like a gun, loaded and pointed at his own head. she's down the hall in her prayers, in her psalms, her voice singing some song to the radio in the downstairs bedroom where she sleeps now. everything is rolled into my arms, his boots and gloves, his old work clothes. i'm stepping down into the cellar, down the same eleven steps he stepped. i'm already in hell, some part of him and his darkness, the fluorescent work light like a bug in the air, the furnace pilot and the water heater and the shadow that grows behind them, the water, almost ankle high and across the floor.

his body has gone bad, misshapen and bloated. i don't know what part was the whiskey and what part was the weather, it's been twelve years since i've seen him. all i really know of those years is a spotty history made of greeting cards and obligatory phone calls, years of christmas pictures i keep like a well. year by year the booze pushing out his guts, ripping the rest of him away, leaving him sunken and lined and chewing the sides of his mouth. his life a long death and death seems to become him. it is white and chaste and queerly elegant amongst the chaos of his living. he seems almost young again, filled into his skin, veined like a strange woad marble or a newborn before its first breath. i pull his feet thru the bunched up openings of his pants, drag the duck cloth up his legs under the paper gown they put around him. he's as stiff as a thick oak felled from a wind, twisted like an old branch following a fickle sun. i button his pants, tear the hospital gown away, his chest like an empty box, his belly and ribs.

i've fallen into some leathered corner in my head, some-place dark and folds of skin, the place i went when he was screaming, when she was screaming, when i was a kid. i'd run from the house to the river and to the rock just down from the near bridge and lay in the sound of the water and the woods and the daft of my own breathing, the nothing of the birds in the trees. it was the rock ledge where i fell into the air, into the river, what seemed the whole earth and the start of my life, the easy current of my death, a relief from the wool of their voices and my thoughts, thoughts when i was young when i should've been just dreaming. i'm not thinking now, i can't. i'm dreaming like when i'm really working, unconscious, any genius is only the aftermath of a perfect mistake. i'm only watching, looking at myself from across the room, looking at him like a sample in a jar. i start the sleeve of his flannel shirt up his arm, his body too rigid to ever get his t-shirt on, pulling the rest of the flannel behind his back and beneath him. i start the other sleeve, i'm afraid i'm going to break him again, his broken leg pushing out oddly at his pant leg to remind me. and somehow it's done. i button his shirt as if it mattered, straighten his collar, roll up his sleeves to his elbows and start the saw.

"james? what are you doing dear? james?"

her voice is in my dream and outside of me, beyond this sort of sleep and the blur around my apple eye. everything is green, the green button on and the whirr of reality, a

large red button next to it that will end it all, the crafts-
man table saw, the sun center of his workshop. it's where
everything started and stopped, the saw blade starting,
spinning, almost ringing, the noise from its motor the hum
of pure destruction like the wrath good of god and his
way. this moment is the sum of my past and his past, the
complexity of our lives and the simplicity of a single act,
the pass of a saw blade, what we keep and what we let go.

i stand back for a moment, standing in the water and in
some big scheme of things, watching the whirl of the table
saw and all the evidence of our brevity, how small the two
of us have become, the universe expanding out and away
from us, leaving us only atoms to spin around ourselves. i
roll the gurney next to the work bench, one hand on the
blade handle, the other hand on his hand, a clean cut, skin
and muscle, tendon and bone. i put his right hand in an
old bread bag he saved for god knows what, schwebel's rye,
what he always ate. i'm working now, making something
by taking it away, it's not what's there, but what isn't there,
it's what sculptors do, but i'm not thinking.

"james, are you okay, dear?"

she's calling down the stairs like you'd whisper into the
dark thinking there's somebody there and not really
wanting an answer and never trusting the silence after

anyway. she'll keep calling, i won't listen, but i'll hear her and remember, but we all scratch at our scabs until we're satisfied that we've made ourselves bleed. i turn the gurney around, lay his other arm on the table, plumb the saw arm, let the blade do its work, deliberately like he taught me, his arm cut clean and straight thru. i leave the saw on, its motor hum my mantra. i am pure, saintly, sharpened and calibrated, a straight cut myself.

"james? james, john and tim are in the driveway, should i send them down?"

i'm pushing old hamburger from the garbage pile into his gloves, the smell, like his body, is edged with decay. i wrap the glove cuffs to the stub end of his arms with bailing wire, around enough so i know they won't slip, pull his flannel shirt sleeves down over his gloves, turn the saw off and awake from this sort of dream i'm sleeping.

"now they can burn you."

i utter the words like a last prayer, like a profanity a priest might whisper under his breath, a last rite maybe and a birthright, our communion, our communion done. i cover him with the sheet again, vespers, compline, matins.

"james!"

"yeah mom..."

"john kapelka and tim are here."

"yeah come on down... i was just trying to clean things up... be careful guys the steps are tricky."

20

they say indians lived along the sides of the river, it's just one of those things you pick up when you're a kid and keep and never really think about like a chicken pox scar. the only signs of them now are buried in the mud, arrowheads and grinding stones, bones once when they were digging the foundation for the high school, an indian's profile painted on the gymnasium wall. my father was alive once, his life dug into this cellar, the river in clear glass sample jars, brown bottles of bourbon whiskey, the old console black and white that sat in front of his chair. it's our life now, his truck on its axles on blocks in the back, what he left me, what i'll remember and put into the earth. but life is hard and this truth is even harder, when i look hard between the trees and see what really happened. he drank himself here, down into this dark, but death is easy and shadows are abundant in this part of the country. some things i know, i know he's dead, i've never met an indian.

they're in coats, the two of them, the temperature dropping, it will this time of year, the fringe of winter still. burger-meister has a jeans jacket over his flannel shirt, it smells of cigarettes and gasoline, the vague, stale smell of the heater, his smell even before him, four steps ahead of him down the stairs. kapelka is in the suit he wore to church and a nylon parka jacket over that so he looks like he's wearing everything he owns. he's showered and shaven, his hair parted and combed, dial soap and bryllcreem, listerine and brut aftershave. all his smells between every other smell so i have to swallow hard or be sick on his shoes.

"will you look at all the shit down here... jesus christs!"
"tim, please, watch your language."
"somethin' down here is pretty ripe, whew..."
"timothy!"
"i think i'm gonna need a drink before we do this."
"you're driving!"
"hey! guys... easy."
"i'm sorry james... how are you?"
"it's been a couple of really long days, man. i don't think any of it's even sunk in yet."
"it takes time. is your father's body okay? it was pretty warm yesterday."

"yeah, he's not too bad i guess."

"thank god it cooled down, the weather is saying clear and cold tonight..."

"shit, that goddard guy on five don't know dick, anyhow, i bet it rains for another two weeks."

"don't worry tim, you'll have the business, town is down-stream, it's always the last to dry."

"can't last long enough for me, better money than a good snow."

"so are we ready?"

i pull the sheet back from his body like a magic act.

"jesus christ!"

"timothy! wait for us upstairs."

"what?"

"please, why don't you get the truck ready while james and i take care of his father, it's better that it's family anyway."

"you're not family."

"i'm a mortician, this is my job... tim, please."

"i don't give a shit, you do it kapelka, the whole thing is creepy anyway."

burgermeister sulks up the stairs, he was always picked last to play.

"i'm sorry about all this. he's an idiot, but his truck is the only thing that's going to get us there, i guess that's not very christian of me, but..."

"don't sweat it, it's all a bit weird, and what's even weirder is it doesn't even seem weird anymore."

"i'm sorry james i didn't really follow you."

"never mind... i mean do you ever get used to it? do you even think about them anymore? i mean when you're dealing with a body."

"of course, i think about death every day, it's what i do."

"yeah, but does it ever get normal?"

"death is normal."

"you know what i mean, i mean does it... i mean are you..."

"no."

"no what?"

"no, i'm not afraid of death, if that's what you're asking."

"well yeah, i guess. i'm not sure if i'm afraid or not, i think about it... probably more than i should."

"everybody thinks about death, but it's just a thought until they experience a real loss, until then they don't know. i've been around death my entire life, it's an everyday thing for me."

"that's what i mean."

"but i don't take it lightly, yes, everything dies, but it's still a loss that's to be understood and... respected, i think respected is the word."

"i want to ride with him."

"absolutely, timothy's truck has a bench seat, i'm more than happy to sit in the middle, i ..."

"i want to ride in the back with him."

"we didn't put the cap on."

"that's fine."

"it's going to be pretty cold back there, this isn't california."

"i guess you've never spent a summer in san francisco."

"no."

"don't worry."

"it's up to you, i'm here to service you and your family."

"i just feel like i should be with him."

"well, there's no right or wrong way, you do what you have to do."

"thanks, i need to see him all the way thru this... i've come this far, you know."

"yes you have, i'm sure your father would be proud of you... how's your mother holding up?"

"she never misses a beat, you saw her at church."

"she's a very strong woman."

"well whatever... you call it strength, i say delusional."

"faith is a powerful thing, james. don't underestimate your mother."

"you don't know her like i know her."

"well i guess i could say the same, you haven't been home for twenty years."

"twelve."

"well twelve years... your mother is very well thought of at saint joseph's, she's done a lot of good for a lot of people."
"that's great, i'm glad."

there's an awkward silence, only the sound of water running down a black metal drain pipe from the kitchen sink above, her paddy cake feet on the floor boards and finally her voice from the door at the top of the steps.

"is everything okay john?"
"yes mrs. tully, everything is fine, we're preparing to move mr. tully right now! would you like a few moments with your husband before we take him out to the truck?"
"i've said my goodbyes, john."
"of course, yes... um, james, are you ready?"
"yeah, let's do it."
"you dressed him?"
"it seemed like the thing to do."
"you were thorough, gloves even."
"i thought it might keep him from spoiling sort of, you know if i wrapped him up ... i didn't know what to do ... at least it kept the flies off him."
"you did a good job, dressing is not easy, his body must be pretty rigid by now."
"yeah, i couldn't get his t-shirt on."
"there's a trick to it... well if things don't work out for

you in california you can come back and work with me."

i look at kapelka blankly like i'm still in my dream, maybe i am. i wonder what my mother told him. i'm worried he'll notice his hands, his broken leg, his shoulder, everything about the old man's body that is wrenched and wrong.

"i was just kidding, a little mortuary humor."
"oh yeah, sorry... you know i broke up with my fiancée wednesday night, the same goddamn night my father died."
"i'm sorry."
"she'd moved out a couple of months ago, but i never thought it was over, i always thought we were going to get back together, like it was some phase we were going thru or something."
"it's hard."
"fuck it, it doesn't matter, my life has always been ... i don't even know what, my life is just fucked."
"god never hands us more than we can hold. you'll get through this and be stronger, you'll survive."
"yeah i know, i always do, at least that's what i keep getting told."
"see, praise god."
"yeah."

i don't know why i told him, sometimes a stranger is the safest place, i guess. some strung afternoon bartender cutting limes before happy hour and it's just the two of you, the lunch crowd left or a woman not pretty, but open faced, in the next seat on the plane, someone who doesn't know you and has a chance to understand.

"okay james, we better get going, are you going to be all right?"
"yeah."
"he seems strapped in tightly... ready?"
"yeah."
"on three..."

kapelka and i fold the gurney down, raise him up off the floor and out of the water, his weight up the stairs. there are eleven steps, there always has been, the cellar behind us and its hem, the hall smells of her and her candles and thru the house. everything is like i knew it would be, the four porch steps, the last steps in the gravel to the back of the truck. we lay his body down under the sky, tie the gurney to the sides and step back and look things over like we just dug a hole.

we'll be out on the river road when it will hit me and years from now when i get it, the dark and just how clear it was, how the highway was waiting. but for now i can't see a thing, but you can't see the river moving when you're in it, you only see the banks passing by like it's somehow the fault of the land. i can't keep him, i couldn't keep nik, i never had them, just breaths i had to let out if i'm going to live and breathe in again.

"i need to grab a coat."

my breath out into the air. i walk inside the house, it seems somehow darker than the night, the supperless lights only making it harder to see. his dun canvas work coat on the broom closet door knob where he hung it, the same duck as his pants, lined and torn, worn ragged on the inside, acetate and rayon. the duck is stiff and good, a man's cloth and at the elbows and soft corduroy at the collar so not to chafe your neck. it is a man's coat, a two day beard.

"james?"
"yeah mom?"
"are you going with john and tim?"
"i'm going with dad."
"i'm glad, he would have liked that, your father hated being alone... it's a funny thing, he'd scream and yell at me that i was never home and when i was home he'd tell me to leave him alone."
"i don't know, mom... it's all hard to understand, i don't think we ever will."

"oh, it's okay, i know your father loved me, he loved us both, that's all we have to know."

"yeah... i guess... we'll probably get back pretty late, so i'll see you in the morning."

"i'll wait up, i have a thousand things to do around here and anyway..."

"mom, you've got a big day tomorrow and it's been pretty stressful, you should get some rest."

"you sound just like your father, but i've got..."

"mom, please go to bed, you've got to take care of yourself."

"okay, okay i'm going to bed, right after i call judy, i've got to call judy and then i'll go."

"we don't have a phone, mom."

"i brought one from church, kate bender, she's such a lovely person went home and got it and brought it back, it's one of those new phones."

"a new phone?"

"one of those walkie talkie phones."

"a cordless?"

"i'm not sure... see."

"mom, it's a cordless phone, that's what it's called."

"boy if your father saw this."

"mom, you're going to get sick if you don't get some rest."

"i'm fine, go... i'll be in bed before ten."

"all right, i can't argue with you anymore, bye."

"bye, bye, i love you."

"...i love you, too."

i raise my foot on the bumper to get in the back. i can hear the two of them, their voices in the truck's cab like drums. i can't understand them, but i know they're arguing.

"if he's comin' he's payin', no one rides free... it's a hundred there and a hundred back, for both of 'em, him and the stiff."
"timothy, show some respect."

i feel a history of blood beneath my face, a cold rising from the well in me, where i keep it, what makes me curl my hands into a fist and my eyes turn like a screw, my feet on the gravel just as hard. i walk around to burgermeister's window and open his door. he looks shocked. he knows he flinched, he wonders if i noticed. he tries to get himself right, as tall as his trailer park pride will push his shoulders up and his stupid chin out. he steps down out of the truck because he has to.

"i'll tell ya what, burgermeister, you get us there and back and i'll pay you a hundred and fifty for the both of us."
"james, you shouldn't have to deal with this, it's the mortuary's responsibility to transport your father, i'll..."
"bullshit, it's my truck and i say what's what... four hundred!"
"i only have a hundred and eighty on me."
"four hundred, cash."

"come on, my mom already paid you good money to get her to church."

"if you've got yourself some other way to get up the river road then do it. otherwise it's gonna be four hundred. i'm not chargin' kapelka cuz he's dealin' with the stiff... i ain't gonna touch him, that's the deal."

"burgermeister, if you refer to my father one more time as a stiff, i'm gonna rap an ax handle around your ass."

"go on boy, i ain't scared..."

"enough! both of you, it's holy saturday..."

she's on the front steps standing straight, almost angled forward out of the porch boards, alabaster as the plaster madonna in the garden she pours bleach on to keep the lichens off. her red hair on her head and grayer than i remember, her eyes green even in the dark, her blind eye, the porch light behind her, a fury of moths at the bulb.

"...timothy burgermeister, mr. tully gave you all those parts for sweetheart from his old truck in the back. i think four hundred is a fair price for those parts, don't you?"

"i ..."

"and all those times he took you and richie petrovsky fishing to his secret spot... you never caught so many fish, no one knew the lake like mr. tully. i suggest you get in that truck and drive and i'll say a prayer for your forgiveness!"

burgermeister thinks to speak, but he says nothing, his head spinning like a loose fan belt. he tries to look at her, he looks at me, the same look he'd shrug at a teacher when he got busted smoking in the john. he's a small, thin man like the filterless cigarettes he smokes, smoked down and smaller now. he has bad skin, oily and acned, almost adolescent, he was thirty-one last august. he taps a pack in his palm, pulls one with his lips and lights it with a yellow disposable lighter. he tries to look cool, blowing the smoke straight out as if to say something. it's all he's ever really said. he'll curse and talk tough later, down at the townhouse, it's what the townies do. he won't say a word for now. i can feel him get back in the truck and sit down heavily, i'm done looking at him, i'm only listening, the engine starting, angry with air and too much gas, gravel spraying out and into the wheel wells, the night pushing in around us and filling into the space where we just were.

i lean my back against the truck cab, the gurney beside me, the sheet we tied to him flapping in the wind. i turn my head up and at the trees that grow across the river road and at the night sky hanging in their branches. all the stars and a lopsided moon caught in the leaves like a strange fruit only the birds can eat, like the red berries he told me to never pick. all those years riding in the old man's truck and years ago, a truck bed befitting for his last ride, more than the hearse, i'm sure. it's like old times, him and me on the river road and the river alongside us like our broken childhoods, what winds its way thru our lives and thru the trees to town and to the lake waiting like a well of souls. this stretch of the river is old and the lake a long story with only an end, the parts we knew and thought of as ours. we're headed east now, towards the gas station town and to the highway fifteen minutes past to the city, what's on some strange part of the lake like someone you know and never really know, the nice boy next door with eight bodies in the basement freezer chest. the beginning of the river is somewhere this side between the long woods and a rise before the highway, the part of the road that was unknown to us, but it's hard to know where things get started. it seems everything just comes out of the ground here, what appears without reason, but for the pressure of water behind it.

it's all happening without me, the highway north to the south shoulder of the lake, the factoried city and the gray they make there. the highway sky is tied with power lines and a telephone line maybe, something humming with a million lives from one wire, but there is only the truck's tires on the dry pavement and the air at this speed. the drone has deafened me and wove me into a spell and a sort of silence kept to vacant parking lots, the asphalt at the end of the road. what became of the highway is finally just a crease between the warehouses and the factories and the barges quiet biding. this is a working lake and a steel town, coal and limestone coke, hard folk like cast iron, breaking before they bend.

there is a brick building among the brick buildings and smoke stacks, below the avenue bridge and the acetylene eyes of the great lake electric company. there is a cov- eralled man i'll never meet waiting to take my father's body in thru a double steel door. he'll take a bite of a corned beef sandwich and add the old man's name to a clip board in black letters, t-u-l-l-y and burn him easter sunday morning. kapelka will bring him back in a black plastic can the next day as planned and be done.

she and i will have to wait and for his smell to fade into the paint, for the flood to recede to wet patches and mud, for his end and ashes. we'll pour him into the emptiness come monday and carry the rest of his weight around until it pulls us into the ground as well. and someday, maybe, i'll throw her into the wind where she can escape into the air like a rain, but even rains fall and become part of the earth again, part of this everything and something i can't divine or follow.

21

the earth echoes with us and with everything before us, the sound below every sound, the hum
buzz of nothingness. yet god wrenched a whole world out
of nothing, from what she told me when i asked and where
the river started, "everything comes from god, james". the
old man sat in the cellar and drank and sadly pondered
my little questions like i had a plastic bag over my head
or over his head. he said how nothing is a big word and
that everything is made of atoms and atoms are mostly
nothing, that it's the space between things that makes them
useful. i think about that still. i still don't know about god,
but i know we'll all fall from our feet to the earth and turn
to nothing again. and then there's the rumor of a jesus
coming up out of the ground like a well spring or a daffodil
and maybe i don't know a thing.

it's sunday easter morning, even the sun has risen, the old man is still lying in a steel metal drawer. if he had got up he'd be drinking instant coffee, gulping vodka to stop the shaking, wringing his hands like he did and reading yesterday's paper like it was today's. he drank vodka in the mornings thinking we wouldn't know, i never knew any different, it's how the morning smelled and pop tarts and frosted flakes, anything she wouldn't have to make, what she'd only have to open. if she knew, she never said a word, she only hurried off to morning mass waving from the gravel road like peoples wave in parades, always really waving goodbye and never waving hello. maybe the old man was right and it was about the space between things, all of us at our ends and the neverness of love and death and wireless phones. and maybe the smell we smelled in the morning wasn't the vodka, but the brown booze after all, the bourbon whiskey he drank every night starting just past four. the coveralled man will burn him in a couple of hours and he'll be mostly space like he said. i guess he would've known the chemical equation for turning his skin and bone into carbon and calcium, the energy required. nothing is a big word.

"rejoice, christ is risen! ... james darling are you awake?"
"what?"
"happy easter, dear."
"mom, last night was pretty intense... the whole easter thing is a little more than..."

"oh! i've got a card for you and nicole somewhere... well for you, i don't know where it got to."

"that's okay, mom."

"i'll find it later..."

"mom, do you think we could ever have a conversation in the same room instead of screaming across the house."

"you stay in bed, i'm just going to say goodbye from down here, i'm in a rush to get ready for the 7am mass. tim burgermeister is picking up the entire choir for easter mass, he and his brother put an old couch in the back of sweetheart so we can all sit."

"that's great, mom."

"i want to meet him out at the near bridge to save some time... i told him i'd meet him at 6:15."

"mom, you're paying this idiot a fortune, the least he can do is pick you up at the house."

"saint joseph's is paying for the entire thing...only eight of us need a ride, evelyn and suzanne and jill and john angellogetti and..."

"mom, please don't go thru the whole list."

"oh, and gerald ravlocovich, god bless his heart, he's eighty-nine, he was singing in the choir before i was born."

"mom!"

"well anyway, the rest live in town and can get there on their own."

"i was hoping we could talk about tomorrow."

"i'll be gone all morning... and i'm helping serve the easter brunch. i'm just sick about those pierogies going to waste."

"mom, dad just died don't you think maybe you should take it a little easy."

"people are going to be asking where the pierogies are, i'm just going to have to tell them that your father made over two hundred and forty pierogies and that they were ruined in the electrical blackness..."

"blackout, mom, it's a black-out."

"yes, blackout... and that your father is dead and that's just the way it is, i'm sorry, but there's no pierogies."

"jesus."

"what? darling."

"nothing, mom."

"i'm leaving now dear... happy easter, i'll bring you back a plate of goodies... wait until you try sarah kozlowski's apple strudel, i think it's as good as your grandmother's, it's a pascoula recipe, it's just to die for!"

"better than the jello?"

"the weather is absolutely beautiful, look at that easter blue sky, god always blesses us with such lovely weather on easter, i hope you'll get out and enjoy it."

"mom, it's really early, i need to sleep some more... i was hoping we could talk about a few things later today."

"james, did you see my purse lying around somewhere? where is that purse...?"

"mom... i'm sorry."

"it's okay i found it."

"i mean i'm sorry for everything... dad and everything that happened."

"we'll talk later, dear, i have to go, i love you... rejoice, rejoice!"

her voice is in the air even after she's left like the lasting effect of a high childhood fever. she heard me, but she won't listen and she surely won't forgive me, "only god can forgive us, james." she'll never forgive him, if she did she'd have to forgive herself, give up her guilt and her genuflects, accept the idea that we deserved better. maybe god needs her more than she needs him, i wonder if god would exist without her. they say he gave up his only son for our sins, a center ring stunt to keep her around. that's the way i see it, but i'm a jealous man. the old man only waded in the river, he never walked on it, walking on the carpet in his dirty shoes, every night in the dark, drunk in his chair. and me upstairs with my g.i. joes in a line and my dirty clothes under the bed, all my prayers under my breath. what could we ever do to top god's trick and what she gave to god in return.

she won't ever see what happened, the high wires and hollers, the broken bottles in the sink, but faith is believing without looking and nothing ever happened looking out her right eye. some part of her knows, it's her natural right, we've chewed all our food and i love her anyway. i'll always love her, love him, no matter what, it's what we do, all of us, regardless of the drunks and rages, all the nights she was gone. it's bred into us, into me, and wound around our spines. it's what raises us up, the love and how love eats away at our sides till there's nothing left, and nothing is the work of god.

i'm floating in my dandelion head, a bee bouncing against the window screen, drunk with the morning's heat, it's hot again. his hands are in the cellar in an old bread bag in the freezer. they're waiting for me like a late life suicide, something i was always going to do. there's some part of me that's killing me faster than time, some disease i was born with, something i got from him and gave to every woman i've loved. i've run down my whole life until i've reached this bottom, it's what water does until it stops. i watch the bay from up and down the hills, from between the buildings and the bridge, from the apartment where nik and i lived. i wonder if it watches me, if it's waiting, if it knows. i wonder if the old man knew, if the bourbon stared back at him. he'd tell me you can know where a river ends without ever knowing where it starts, that most answers just leave you with more questions than before. i'm forty and i don't know a damn thing, but suicides and women will do that.

i can hear the river or my blood, maybe the hot water heater filling up. i sit up off the bed springs, i don't remember even getting into bed. i remember the back of burgermeister's truck though and the empty gurney on the way home, how big the night felt and how far it felt between things. there was a moon two hundred thousand miles away, its reflection right in the river and a fog amongst the trees along the road and nothing i could touch. i wondered where nikki was right then and how far her long hair fell, if she saw the same moon as me and maybe whispered my name or his. i started out just wanting to love her, but i needed her instead. and need will turn on you, eventually, and leave you wanting and nothing more.

i need to know some part of him, some piece of my life from beginning to end, something i can believe even if my memories are becoming just stories. i can't have him ash and smoke, smoke is of the air and the air is for angels. he and i are no angels, water and earth make mud. i'll put his hands in the ground, pull this nothingness together, some forever or the river. and maybe it's a sin, more than living this life, but rivers always know their end, lakes or oceans, something bigger than them and better.

i can't sleep anymore, i can't swim that long, these dreams up over my head. the day is all the way into my room, the sunlight muddled on the walls like the crayon marks still there from when i was a kid. i hadn't noticed them before, he painted over them like my childhood in the same yellow paint. in the sunlight they show thru, a dig of scribble and stick figures with big round heads and sunshines and rain clouds and a crooked red house. i'm up standing naked at the window, i close my eyes, let them run red against the real sun, let the light fall across my skin, hoping it will fill me back in again at the hole in my side where i gave myself away. nik will always own a piece of me, a sad smile she won't know she's wearing and me with a missing tooth. i'm a little less each time, each one of them. someday there will be nothing left of me or for this life to root to, like one of the big trees that finally tumbles into the river. i'll fall like he fell, into a mystery and misunderstood.

i put on clean underwear thinking about what she always said when i was a kid about clean underwear and what if i have to go to the hospital. i pull my jeans on like he taught me, humbly, one leg at a time, another t-shirt, a faded giants ball cap. i tie my boots deliberately like it means something and walk downstairs past her altars to the kitchen and the picture christ tormented on the kitchen wall.

"today's your big day, man."

i'm talking to myself, to the wall christ, to the rusting ceiling light, i guess i've always been talking to god, hoping he's listening, a whole life of talking out loud alone in one long prayer. i'm looking for something to eat or some sort of faith, something to change my mind. i can't seem to find either.

"fucking burgermeister!"

he's eaten what was left of the leftovers. i suppose it's best to be hungry, i imagine jesus was hungry in the end from the looks of it.

"thirty three and you never knew a woman... i guess i never knew any of them either..."

i rinse out a cup from yesterday and take a drink of water from the tap. it smells like the lake, like fish, it always did in the summer. the old man would hold up a sample vial and say something about acceptable levels of organic substances, she just said it stank. i hold my breath and swallow the rest like a whole lifetime and head down the hall for the cellar steps and the end of any ideas i might have had about him and easter.

the water on the cellar floor has settled into several large puddles, the air is heavy and smells of mildew and maybe him. i push my tongue between my teeth, open the freezer door like the hearse's doors, his hands amongst a donnybrook of plastic sample bags and plastic jars, everything thawed and frozen again, found out secrets of the lake and the river, secrets that will stay with him.

i take out his hands and lay them on his work table like the samples he took from the river. i set them so the fingers from each hand are almost touching and think about the space between things and how far i am from anyone i've loved. i open up his lab notebook, a three ring binder with green lined graph paper, and turn past the numbers and the sum totals to an empty page. i sit where he sat, on the metal stool that's always been there and begin to sketch his hands with a cheap blue bic pen. he used blue ink so he knew between originals and copies. he used bic pens because that's what he took from the state regulatory office. his hands are bloodless and beautiful, almost white like a first winter field dusted with snow. there's dirt under his fingernails, he would have wanted it that way. i stare down at my hands, at his hands, at what i've drawn. it's not the lines that are important, but the nothingness between them, it's not our hands, but what they hold. it's the god in us i guess, that sees the nothing as something, the lines we connect, the space we fill so we feel whole.

i put his hands back in the schweibel's bag and take them up the cellar steps to the living room, the four boxes filled with the pieces of his life stacked on the coffee table there. i gather everything under my arms, all that's left of him, what's left of me and start towards the door. i move across the room no different than the dust floating thru the bands of light struck from the window, quietly appearing in the sun and disappearing in the shade again. my boot steps on the musty carpet, on the porch boards, across the river rocks to the shed, a long spade and a maddox over my shoulder, the grind of the gravel road, the sun ninety two million miles away and somehow here between the trees.

my head is filled with a cracker jack idea, a dark thought enough to turn the weather. i wonder what nikki would do if i did it, if i did myself like the old man done. maybe she'd never know or she'd hear years later and go home and throw up, sitting all night with her arms folded and a heating pad across her stomach like she does. maybe she'd walk by our old apartment and look up in the window thru the grate of the fire escape, pretend she's looking at the sky or sit on the bench seat along the window at the trieste with some knitting pin notion spinning in her head until it would be a secret even to her and think of me. maybe she'd wonder why, but she'd know why, that's why i loved her.

i know my mother would cry, mary cried marble and wood paint, cast plaster in the yard and on the church walls. she'd cry, but for herself and for "her son," she wouldn't cry for me. and she'd pray and light candles and play her music on the radio and everyone at church would say how sorry they are and how strong she is and whisper the word suicide like a shadow and how could he do it, both of them, what a shame, she deserved better. she'd say it was god's will, the old man said there was no use swimming upstream. the women from the choir would bring her casseroles and the jello mold she loves and all the parishioners would take a certain solace in her suffering and an age old satisfaction in her loss. we all need a martyr, most of all believers, even the good people at the saint joseph's catholic church.

i wonder... but i won't.

22

the water has made its way underground and to the secrets there, indian bones and thoughts of snakes, all the things we can't bring ourselves to think about. i can feel the river a quarter mile from the near bridge like i'd feel him sitting downstairs in the dark in his chair. the water angry with weeks of rain and the grade, him burning so black he made the night black, the rattle of an ice cube in his glass like something waiting. you can hear the river for miles, if you're quiet, if you listen, a tatting of its sound amongst every other sound, something that was a part of my sleep and somehow the sound of him. i can't help but hear it, i want to believe, we all want to know god, and god and death are the same.

the river has waned, but just below the '36 mark on the bridge, its bell still ten feet above the normal. the old man would have said that there's no such thing as normal, that there's only averages and median points and that they're just math and never the truth. he'd say people are always trying to make something out of the nothing between things, that things fall everywhere but the middle, that the true nature of things are at their edges. he'd say things like that and drink till he was at his own edge and passed out in his chair.

i'm at the bank of the river, the beginning of the near bridge, the calamity of the current upon the clay dirt and roots and the rock worn to stones at the sides. i hesitate before i start across, everything edged up against me so there's hardly room to move, the sun all around my shadow and right up to my skin. everything is pushing to the corners of my eyes. everything is morning new and new born, blue and just green and alive again, the river brown again like a strange girl's skin and heavy with all the mineral elements of the earth and its sadness. the air is a puzzle of vert smells and bird songs, last year's leaves drying in the sun, the stew of the river and what the rain left or took away. and somehow i am a part of this and everything and everything is richer and brighter and louder like the first time i saw a color t.v. i was seven i think or would be that end of winter. the old man had taken me to the higbee's in the city to see a santa, to the terminal tower building where you could see across the lake to canada if it was clear. it rained, it almost snowed, yet everything was suddenly different and three colors and for the first time i could see where i was just looking before. the old man would drive us back home that night and to the guile of my eyes, to his eyes and hers and a fourteen inch black and white that was really just gray, but i would ever after know gilligan's shirt was red and the skipper's, blue.

i stop half way across the bridge and look over into the river. i'm almost nothing, only atoms on the other side of this rail, the water waiting, the river no different than the bay. i wonder if it's the same water, if it's following me or if i'm, maybe, following it, if it wants to kill me or if i want to die. it's hard to know who will get their way. i won't lose whatever end i have left, i won't let him fall to just ashes. i've come this far, to the edges like he said, the middle a matter of the farthest points. i move on across the near bridge towards the other side. the rumble of the water beneath me like a regret i've grown used to, a roofing nail i'm too superstitious to pull from the thick of my boot sole sounding on the cement to remind me each step, the sound of my steps on the golden gate, on the sidewalk up lombard, up jones, when she loved me, when i was in the middle or on the other side of this side.

i step off the bridge back onto the gravel road and to the left, the way i remember, down a grown over path thru the prickers and several points past to the rock ledge where our deaths first started. there are rises of dirt, sinew and blood veins running under the earth and wove thru the humus of the woods. there are rucks of stones up out of the leaves, river rocks stacked and fallen and some not fallen, but standing like a few good memories. i don't know which were by his hands and which were by mine or chippewa's. there seems there was never a time before them. they taught us in school that some of the mounds were a thousand years older than jesus and built by some sort of peoples before the indians even. my father was born in 1936 just after the flood.

he took me on a car trip one summer, a billboard vacation, a sunday and south on the highway to the biggest river in the region and to the biggest indian mound in the world. he said the ohio drained some seventy percent of the state, that its waters run all the way to the ocean. the great serpent mound stretches out a quarter mile or more, its open mouth eating a separate mound that is an egg. that's what the great serpent mound state park pamphlet said. i thought it might be a river swallowing up the sun or a river running right off the earth like a runaway train, depending on which end was the end and which was the beginning. the old man liked the idea of that and asked a brown booted man what evidence they had that it was a snake and an egg. the man didn't seem to have an answer, but he had a badge and a stripe down his pants and a

strange hat and a way about him that made me think he
didn't know a thing beyond the park's hours. the old man
walked me around the mound and read the signs out loud.
he read that scientist hadn't found a single artifact or bone
in the great mound, that there was nothing in it, but the
clay and stone from the area, that the scientist weren't sure
what it was for. he said it didn't sound like they knew much
of anything, that nothing was always more a mystery than
something unknown. and he told me to ask questions and
to never believe what i was told. he said the truth's most
often the simplest thing in the world and when it's said
and done, the hardest thing to say.

we walked back to the car and he opened a canned beer
and we drove away into the heat waving off the blacktop.
he drank schlitz beers the whole way home searching for
some truth of his own, i guess, or some way to forget it.
i crawled over the front seat into the back and slept as
the night crept over the new fields from the side of the
highway. he had the windows rolled down and all the stars
and a summer in the purple air blowing in, his cigarette
smoke out his mouth, his face and his hands green from
the dash light and yellow, almost white, as a truck or a car
passed by the other way.

i built my own mounds for hours and days after that,
young summers and seasons easily forgotten. i never wondered why or why i stopped, but that's the luxury of youth

and a shady thick of wood. i played indian in between or dreamed of tearing thru a defense, running between the trees like jim brown thru a team of tacklers and too close to the river bank. i was testing the edges of life and death and life really, brandishing all the cunning of a child, a brutality only innocence and imagination can breed. i knew about nothing then and did it all day and all of it was my secret and the good smell of getting away with something, the myrrh of the river and the woods and a faith that i've surely outlasted.

i set his tools and the boxes down at the rock ledge, keeping hold of the bread bag and his hands, and walk thru the limbs and leaves away from the river into the trees. there are stones stacked everywhere, stacked up to knee high, a few even higher like the remains of a stone wall once, time and lichens all about them. they are crooked circles and spirals and odd lines and just piles. they are part of my memory like a rain to the ground, something i don't have to think about, but a part of me like a tooth or a lock of hair. they are part of nature and unnatural, solemn and beautiful and without reason, but beauty is its own reason and something that never makes sense, since men stood up and away from the earth or noticed a woman walk away.

i'm putting the stones back from where they've fallen away from the wall. i don't know why, i only know i will. they feel right in my hands. their weight and their fit fill me where i'm empty like a solid meal or a good sleep after a day's work, like an innocent man eats and sleeps i suppose, i couldn't know. i miss the work though, even the union job welding for caltrans, pulling the space between things together, purposeful tools, my hands on the handles, solder and smoke, the smell of burnt steel. a man is what a man does, that's what the old man would say. it seems even god had to make things.

i find out a flat sharp stone the size of a spade from a pile of stones and head back to the rock ledge, stopping a few feet before, kicking the ground, looking for a soft spot. i kneel down and start to dig, the first part i want to do down close to the dirt. it smells brown and almost black, of roots and rotting leaves, the richness of life each death leaves behind. the ground is sodden with the rain it's kept, the stone pulling the dirt away with ease, the sun hard thru the trees and thru the break in the trees where the river runs. i'm up to my elbows, down on my knees, sweat is running down my back and off the end of my nose. i'll finish with the spade, cutting thru the tough clay and tree roots. i'll work till i forget, forget everything and be only what i'm doing.

the hole is dug, it's as deep as i can dig. it's waiting quietly, a puddle of water in the bottom, in my foot prints to remind me i'll leave a piece of myself here. this is the moment, what i'll remember and somehow change so i can live with it. it's just the two of us now, me and the river and a few pieces of him like these stones that fell away from the wall.

i let his hands fall out of the bag into the space i've dug. i place them so his fingers reach into the ground. i'm sure his hands will grow into trees, but what is any man's grip but the root of something bigger. i put each box in at the sides of the hole imagining some scientist digging them up three thousand years from now. i pull the dirt around them and finally over them, covering them. i watch the last of him disappear, trying to memorize his hands, not looking at the stumps of his wrists where i cut him, trying to picture the lean of his face when he was young, before the booze bloated him and ruined his chin. i stare down at the fresh dirt and the rock ledge and the river some thirty feet below, a birdless sky above everything else, something so blue everything else seems absurd. all i can pray for is quiet, any prayer i had for grace is long gone. i start with a flat stone and another. the earth turns and turns us, last fall's apples in a box in the cellar going soft.

23

some things i've forgotten, maybe, things i only need to be reminded of, of wood rot and mildew and muddied throw rugs. and what i remember, i'll live with and swim in and flail my arms to and drown in, in my dreams and down into my pockets. memories of soft skin and the smell of washed hair, washington square and the sun across an afternoon. memories of her and him, the night all around them, around me and his chair. what i want to forget, what i can't forget, the warning of his glass, her red wig in the sink, dinner burning, its smoke up the stairs, voices raised below the floor, the lonely of car tires on the gravel road till all i can hear is the river, the heartbreak of his whiskey breath goodnight. goodnight.

i'm walking home like i might have been playing in the woods along the river all day, the way i walked everyday when i was a kid. the old house waiting like a new moon, something there that i can't see, but the kitchen light thru the trees and at the end of the gravel road. it's almost dark, the dark is in the woods already. my boots are on the gravel, on the back porch boards. the back screen door hangs on, the bugs are desperate for the light. he's back behind me now, the best part of him, hands that could've done anything. the rest of him smoke and ground bones, what wouldn't burn and someone's turn to scour the crematory.

"james, thank god, you're home, i was getting worried, i was... james! dear, you're absolutely filthy, what have you been doing?"
"i was working on something."
"it's easter sunday."
"and what? it's the sabbath? we were going to have a big easter dinner?"
"it is the holiday."
"please, you were gone all day doing whatever you do. i wasn't going to sit around and wait for you with my nose pressed on the window. i'm not seven."
"i was at holy mass, james, seven thirty, nine and eleven, you make it sound like i'm out goofing around."
"you were doing exactly what you wanted to do, okay, so don't kid yourself that it's some big sacrifice."
"it's about god, james."
"it's about you."

"i have obligations to saint joseph's and to my faith, song and prayer are a very powerful thing, i say prayers for us every day."

"you prayed for dad everyday too and look where it got him."

"your father lost his faith, i prayed that he would find his way back to god before he destroyed himself... now all i can do is to pray for god to have mercy on his soul."

"maybe you should have been home dealing with things instead of volunteering at saint joseph's and hoping god would make it all better."

"there was nothing i could have done to stop your father from drinking."

"you know i lived here too. maybe you could have been home for me."

"well i don't know what all this therapy of yours is doing? why did nicole stop going?"

"nikki has nothing to do with what we're talking about."

"it seems to me you want to blame your entire childhood on your father and me."

"and who exactly do you think is responsible?"

"james, you're never going to move on until you take responsibility for your own childhood."

"oh my god! you know what, lets just drop it, you and i just can't talk, we just go around in the same circle, over and over... i'm not going to get into it with you anymore."

"your father was a sick man."

"mom, we need to plan out the memorial tomorrow and i need to eat something before i turn inside out."

"i don't know why your father drank, he had a very hard childhood, your uncle and your aunts were so much older than him that he grew up almost completely alone."

"mom, enough, please. we've been thru all of this, is there anything to eat in this house?"

"i know you blame me for your father's drinking, but there was nothing i could've done, he was an alcoholic, james, it's a disease."

"mom, let's just drop it, okay, please, let's get tomorrow organized, i'm flying out tomorrow night and i need to get the morning settled."

"so soon?"

"i've been here three days and you've been gone every waking moment, so don't lay some guilt trip on me."

"it's the holy weekend."

"it's always something."

"i thought you'd go thru your father's things."

"i've gone thru his drawer and the cellar as best i could, i took what i wanted."

"i thought we'd spend all of next week together."

"you're so full of it. you want me to clean the house, that's what you want, it would take me a month."

"i know you have to get back to california."

"mom, this is the life you lived in for forty years, you can't expect me to come here and make everything just go away."

"i just wanted to spend some time with you."

"you've had every opportunity to spend time with me."

"i was just telling mary sododi that i was going to spend all day monday with you, i thought you could show me the stuff you want me to put aside for you."

"i'm not going thru that cellar or thru this house anymore than i already have, it's like a sickness and i can't have it around me. it's not like you're suddenly going to go down into the cellar."

"don't be silly, i've been in the cellar."

"when?"

"the boys already said they'd help me with the house and with your father's things."

"jesus."

"what?"

"you never answered me. it's like i'm not even here."

"what do you want me to say?"

"i asked you when you were down in the cellar."

"i don't know exactly when i was downstairs, does it really matter?"

"forget it, let's just talk about dad's memorial."

"you know your grandma mcmullen and i didn't get along till the end of her life. i hated her when i was a child, she whipped me with a willow switch once so bad i bled, your grandpa mcmullen came home from the mill and saw my bottom all bloody and he grabbed her and told her if she ever touched me again he'd beat her to a pulp, that's what he said plain as day."

"mom, let's just try to stay on topic, okay."

"i think our relationship is closer than ever with your father's passing on, that's all i'm saying."

"let's just get thru tonight and tomorrow and not expect too much from each other, okay. i love you and i loved dad, but i can't be in this house, it's too much."

"i love you too, i'm so glad we had this talk and that we have everything settled."

"mom, like i said don't expect too much. can we just talk about tomorrow?"

"you can always talk to me."

"yeah mom... about tomorrow..."

"i finalized everything with father ciolek today at the easter brunch. he's saying mass for your father at nine o'clock."

"why would father whoever say a mass for dad?"

"they're both czech."

" so what?"

"your grandma tully was a hundred percent czech, her maiden name was paskoula which is very czech, it's your grandfather that was from ireland, actually both your grandfathers."

"what are you talking about? i know where my grandparents are from, what does that have to do with you having a mass for dad?"

"your father was raised catholic, besides he made apple strudel for father ciolek every fall when the cooking apples were ready. and boy, did he love it, father said ben made strudel like his mother when he was a boy in bohemia. he never says czechoslovakia, he always says bohemia..."

"dad thought the church was bullshit. let's face it, the mass is for you, which is fine, but let's not pretend any different."

"your father and i discussed this, he said he wanted father ciolek to say the mass and that he wanted it said in latin like when he was a boy."

"you know you've been lying so long i think you actually believe you're telling the truth."

"i've never lied."

"mom, you lied to dad all the time, how many times do you think you told me, 'don't tell your father, it's our secret'."

"i was protecting you."

"you were protecting yourself, you weren't protecting me."

"well i never lied to you."

"you lied to me all the time too. please, you always had some reason why you were late to pick me up from practice or why you didn't come at all... you were always using me for some excuse why you weren't home. i think you lied to me about the cremation, i don't think you had a conversation with dad, i think all of this is your idea."

"i did talk with your father."

"i don't believe you, i never have."

"well i think it's pretty darn sad that you don't trust your own mother."

"don't put that on me, you're not entitled to trust, trust is something you earn."

"well... we're having the reception immediately afterward in the party hall across the lot."

"mom!"

"what dear?"

"what were we just talking about? you just go on like i haven't said a word."

"well you said you didn't want to talk about it anymore, you wanted to know about monday morning, so i'm telling you."

"uhh god..."

"like i said we're having the reception at ten, kathy mcgonigal is making the corned beef and cabbage and roseanne slovinski is making pork feet and sauerkraut and potato dumplings. it's all authentic traditional food, both sides of your father's family should be happy, though your aunt julia is already calling to see if we're going to have the czech carp that your father made with the ginger snaps and the gold raisins. i told her that it was her and ben's mother's recipe and that my husband just died and i didn't have time. she'll probably make it just to try and show me up, which is fine i don't have time for her pettiness."

"who exactly is going to eat this 'authentic traditional' food at ten in the morning? it's disgusting."

"everybody's talking about it, roseanne has been czech her whole life."

"what?"

"kathy mcgonigal married tom, but everybody from saint joseph's knows she's a great cook. she might have been irish before tom."

"i have no idea what you're talking about."

"both roseanne's mother and father were czech, now kathy i'm not sure about, she moved here from erie when she was twenty i think..."

"mom! mom. when are we going to be done with the memorial?"

"we have the hall until noon, then they have to get ready for the kiwanis club."

"okay, so nine till noon."

"yes, i guess."

"have you thought about what you want to do with dad's ashes?"

"john kapelka is making arrangements to have the ashes buried in the tully plot with your grandparents."

"wait a minute. we went thru all this craziness to cremate dad because of all your claustrophobic nonsense and you're going to bury his ashes anyway? i can't even begin to understand you."

"i can't stand the idea of being in that box, james, ughhh..."

"mom, why did you have to have dad's ashes back monday morning for the memorial if you're just going to bury them."

"i thought you'd want some to take with you."

"mom, what am i going to do with some of dad's ashes?"

"your father never saw san francisco and he never got to meet nicole."

"there's a lot of things that didn't get to happen..."

"don't you want some of your father ashes with you? i'll be dead someday."

"mom, why don't we spread dad's ashes out by the river or the lake somewhere, someplace near to home, he should be near to home. this is the only place he's ever been."

"oh james, that is such a great idea, praise god. oh, i know your father would have loved that idea. i'm going to call judy right now and tell her."

"isn't that just common practice?"

"i'm on the phone dear... judy? judy it's me, james and i have been brainstorming ben's memorial and we have come up with such a great idea, it's the power of prayer, praise god..."

i suddenly notice my feet, bones and blue veins that are a mystery to me and somehow mine and just under my skin. i'm in my bare feet, i left my muddy boots on the porch, his boots, my wet socks over the porch rail. i'm standing on the spot on the kitchen floor where the linoleum has worn away, where they stood for what seems a thousand years. i look up again.

"is this what you brought from saint joseph's?"

"hold on judy... james, go ahead and eat, everything there is for you... i brought some goodies for james... i thought the food was excellent this year, did you have evelyn's lemon squares?... they're just to die for... and those 'raviolas' anna scalicci made... well everyone was asking about ben's pierogies..."

there's a brownie and an éclair and a broken sugar cookie that was probably a bunny on a paper plate wedged amongst her other clutter on the kitchen table, the accident of her purse and her glasses, a ridiculous easter hat and a church program, the dare of her lavender scarf hanging over the back of what once was his kitchen chair and the sudden realization that he's really gone. the brownie is like every bake sale brownie, common and sad and fallen from its oven height, the éclair with a bite taken out of it. all of them waiting like a group of poor souls who were just robbed at a bus stop and have to wait for the bus anyway.

i turn around and put my hands under the kitchen faucet, the water falls from the spigot with the effort of something old and old enough to be unsure. it's only when we're young that we really know things. the water and the dish soap sting my hands. i hadn't known the damage i'd done to them. they are ravaged from the rocks, from the digging and the dirt, ten hours of work that's worn the skin away and blistered me under my calluses. my back aches from the large stones, from being bent over, from standing up straight. i watch the water and the dirt spiral down the drain thinking it means something. it should mean something.

i haven't eaten since yesterday, i think. i don't remember when i ate last. there is a little less of me, a little more of me worn away each day, my face reflected in the window above the sink like someone else's face, like something carved out of a shadow and not me. my eyes, sunk in and sallow, like the eyes of the old men that stare out the bus windows, the forty five from work, their other clothes in brown bags in their laps. something has been let out of me and has yet to fill me back in. and if i am empty, maybe i can finally matter. it seems it's the nothingness that matters.

i think to wipe my wet hands on the curtains again, looking over at her on the phone and at the stupid birthday cake smile she wears every day. i wipe my hands on the table cloth instead and fall into one of the three yellow vinyl upholstered chairs around the kitchen table, the same chair i always sat in, but it's the habit of water to run where it did. i bite into the brownie she brought and realize how hungry i am, stuffing the rest into my mouth so that it's gone before i taste it. the cookie the same and matter of fact. i pick up the éclair and examine it like some curious thing i found at the side of the road. i eat it despite the round where her teeth were and the hint of her lipstick around the edge where she bit in. i'm too hungry and too weary to care.

i'm watching her talk on the phone, her head tilted to the base as if it wouldn't work if she sat up straight. i think to tell her she can talk anywhere in the house with a cord-less, but i won't. what could i possibly tell her now? that she didn't need to live like this, between the weak reach of twenty watt bulbs and peeling paint and a sink filled with rotting water that won't drain. it's like holding her blind eye to the sun to see if she can see, something she could never see, something that would only blind her if she did. it's our secret, it's not for the air. she could have gone anywhere, but she stayed.

i feel like i might cry at the sight of her, her bric-a-brac, her trifle and tithe, the narrow of her life and her little chair. i wish i wouldn't have looked. i wish i could've been some jesus for her so her suffering would've mattered, but i'm no son of god, i'm only as sad. i realize now that i love her, i don't want to love her and yet if i only feel sorry for her instead, it's no matter, in this house they were the same. maybe i'll leave here tomorrow and know different, maybe i can let it go, let the rain fall on me and off of me, forget what i could only bear before. and if i can live out this end instead of just dying i'll be one better than him. he never learned to swim and i can at least do a crawl.

"james dear, i'm going to get ready for bed, tomorrow's the big day."
"yeah, i'm tired too."
"goodnight, sweetheart."
"mom, is there anything else to eat? i'm starving."
"i don't know, your father was the cook, i had to throw out all my frozen dinners."
"there has to be something."
"your father didn't really eat anymore... he didn't have any of his teeth, he pretty much just drank, james."
"is there any cereal or something?"
"everything is where it's always been, nothing much changed around here."
"that's for sure."
"goodnight dear."
"goodnight."

she goes down the hall like something broken, something that still works, but won't ever work the same. i can hear her climb up the stairs to the bathroom, the sound of the water in the sink, the toilet, the breath of the dark in and out of the house. i look thru the cupboards for anything to eat, a morton salt in the same old cardboard container, pepper in a rusting metal box, grubby spices in greasy glass jars, a box of corn starch and a baking soda, bags of gravy mix, boxes of jello and tapioca pudding, food coloring from before they knew the red would kill you. behind a jar of instant coffee is a yellowed box of kraft macaroni and cheese. there's probably no milk or butter, but we have water and it will do.

i light the stove with a blue disposable lighter, only the right back burner works of the four. the flame shoots up and out burning the hair on my hand. the smell of something, of sometime when i was young, when i snuck the blue tip matches behind the shed. i put a small bent pan of water to boil and try not to wait. i look over at the phone with a helpless suspicion like the live chickens in the window at the chinese butcher on kearny. i know i'm going to call her, i'm the son of an addict.

my hand is shaking, it's what i'll remember. i dial her number like i have for two years, something as familiar as skin that's become suddenly strange. ten numbers that are some part of her, the only thing i have left of her like the old man's hands out there beneath the stones. her phone rings in the ear piece here, a mystery of electricity and cellular waves, a computer somewhere that hears everything, that's always listening, almost breathing. i won't breathe till it's over.

"hi, this is nikki... i can't take your call right now, please leave me a message and i'll call you back, thank you."

what words are there after goodbye? only words to ourselves, i suppose, squeezed out prayers in the middle of the night, brittle pleas at a naked window, muddled appeals in the streetlight for the neighbors to see. there will be a silence on her voice mail after, the sound of the house and our secrets, the ghosts of their voices, a gossamer of their shouts and screams. i wonder if she'll hear it, the real quiet, if she'll hear the river or if its whispers are only for me.

you hear things over a lifetime, drink your milk, milk builds your bones, safety belts save lives, don't mix your liquors, don't look at the sun, i'll always love you, i love you too. the things people say and don't say. i hang up and dial my voice mail, enter my code...

"you have no voice messages..."

i put the phone down into its base, the water is boiling. of everything said, it seems it's the silence that says the most.

24

before the sun there was the river, some way to the morning before the light. i can hear it now like i listened then, something when there seemed nothing else. the old man would say that all of life started in the water, that the ocean and our blood were the same salt. there was a rhythm here, in the air and to our chests, a beat not ours, but borrowed, some drum of god or the first ocean, maybe, the great lake and the river, what the old man had to finally give back. it is the fabric of this nothingness now. it is the space between us, between here and there, this life and death, canada to the north. that's the river i remember, but my memory has failed me. and maybe the water can forget me and i can live and live out this life without a thought. it's the emptiness that makes the bucket useful.

it's still dark, but i'm awake, it's cold and i don't want to get out of bed. i get up and pull the blanket around me and make my way for the door. i leave the lights off, it's best to leave the lights off, some things are best seen in the dark. i can't see a thing, but i remember the way. i walk down the short hall to the bathroom, my arms inside the blanket, my shoulder against the wall and the peeling wallpaper till i'm at the bathroom door. i close the door behind me before i turn on the light. i drop the blanket so i can piss without risking a mess. for a moment i'm standing naked in the bathroom mirror above the clogged sink, armless and legless, my torso is all that will fit in the frame. i'm almost beautiful like bodies are, stripped stark, a harvested field. i've gone white like something pure or purified, black stubble poking out of my face so i know the days, enough gray to know the years. all that's left of me is above my feet, inside my skin, long bones and luck. i look in the sink, i can't help it, pieces of him floating in the soap scummed water, pieces of her, it makes me want to vomit. i look into the toilet and piss instead.

i wonder if the water will wake her, i flush the toilet any-way. the old man would have left it, saved the water, i always found the bowl filled with piss. she would constantly wail it was disgusting and never think to flush it herself and bang around in the medicine cabinet and hang her blood stained underwear over the shower curtain rod. i just wove between things, but barely, a loose thread, maybe, but part of the yarn.

i look one last time in the mirror like i might write a note to myself, buy tea or remember the dry cleaning, a weekend phone number for hannelore, all of us must sometime be naked. my arms are hung together with gristle and veins, i'm lined at my eyes, my jaw strung tight. i was perfect once, we were, me and you, all of us crystalline and see thru, a pure path to god or good. but the river has worn at me, what the world did to me, what i did to myself, everything that happens to us. all of it has made me blind till i couldn't see or see myself, i couldn't look. now i eat alone, my memory banging the pots and pans down the hall and all night so i can't sleep. everything i want to forget i can't forget, scratching at my scabs till they bleed and fill up my boots. never the memory of my birth or the opportunity of mistakes, maybe the rash chance of love or even forgiveness, but she was only a moment, a good rain that came and went. sometimes i can still smell her hair, my mouth pressed against her temple, the beat of her blood on my lips. maybe i can forgive myself and forget the indian bones, maybe i'll remember my spine instead and where i started, when i was perfect, when we were.

i'm looking in the mirror, i know what i see and that's good enough. i wrap myself back in the blanket, i'm shivering, all my teeth are chattering. i'm not sure that i'm cold. i turn the light off, open the door, feel for the wall and edge myself back to my room. i won't sleep again, not tonight. it will be months from now when i realize i haven't slept thru a night since. i wonder if jesus slept his last night, knowing what he did, if the old man slept, if he knew. i wonder how long it took for the life to leave him, his body left there like an october leaf.

i turn the odd lamp on next to my bed, some part of my childhood and the '60's and seemingly part of this time now. i slip my muddy jeans on from the day before and shudder at their dampness, at the odor of the river and the earth ground into them. i pull on clean socks and a t-shirt and turn the lamp off, closing my eyes hard like i might squeeze the dark out of them. i open them and step down the hall, feeling for each stair, quiet so i don't wake her. i can't hear the river, all i can hear is another kind of silence, the silence of the steps at the center of the house. the pop and crack of the boards like knuckles beneath the carpet, everything seemingly louder because there's no other sound. i am part of the darkness, part of this house, i close her door downstairs without shutting it.

"ben, darling?"

"no mom, it's me."

"the daffodils are lovely, thank you."

"mom, it's me, it's james."

"i never liked roses, mother had a rose garden, she made me weed."

"mom?"

"i always thought the weeds were prettier..."

i leave her to her dreams, to the patchwork quilt her mother left her, a crack of candlelight from under her door, the seven day candles she has burning, the fourth day since his death. i walk down the downstairs hall to the kitchen and switch on the sad overhead light, the light as old as the house, a fixture from '36 and after the '36 flood. i've been thru the cupboards, there's nothing much left to eat, the macaroni and cheese was the last of it. i read thru the nutrition information on a box of jello and a tapioca pudding like i'd look over a chronicle left on a coffee house table. i start some water in the kettle, i'll have the tapioca, i won't wait for it to cool or set.

there's a nether of rain like morning rains are, always close to the earth and for the trees. i can only see it passing by the flood lights shining from the back porch, there's no telling from the ground, the ground has been wet for weeks. at the first chance of light i'll walk back to the woods, back to the river and the rock ledge to see the work i've done. it's work to me, something humble i can put my hands to, art is elusive and most likely an accident, something that happens well after you've walked away. yet art is no more magic than a mechanic turning the timing on a chevy small block or a perfect seam on a tig weld. it's all magic like all this life and living thru it, like this rock and river clay waiting in the woods. it has a life now, it is something more than its elements. it is an arm of me and a leg and beyond me and ending only when i end. and like the old man it will live after its end, between the trees and maybe in people's memories if people ever see it. but it is not for them or even him, it is for me because i have to.

the seeds of the tapioca have swelled and softened enough to eat. it's warm and sweet like kitchen memories can be. i don't think she ever made anything that didn't come from a box.

"james david tully!"
"what?"
"what are you doing?"
"i'm eating breakfast."
"are you wearing those clothes to your father's mass?"
"no, i want to take a walk down to the rock ledge once it's light."
"oh thank god, i thought you were dressed for the memorial. you and that river, your father was no different. tim's picking us up at eight thirty."

"i'll be ready."

"i wanted to ask you which hat you think i should wear. i'll go get them."

"mom, i'm sure whatever you pick out will be fine."

"you've always had such great taste, even when you were young you were very particular, you threw a fit that you didn't get a red bike for your birthday."

"it was purple."

"what dear?"

"it was purple, i wanted a purple schwinn."

"so what do you think?"

"if you're planning on doing a cabaret act, either one."

"i guess you don't know fashion, they were both very expensive hats, james. i bought them at the higbee's downtown, they're from new york."

"i don't know, mom."

"i like this one, i got it on sale for forty five dollars."

"it's fine, mom"

"father and i picked the passages we'd like you to read."

"what?"

"father marked the passages, it's from corinthians, he'd like you to read, in english of course, the rest of the mass will be latin."

"you could have asked me."

"this is what we have planned."

"we?"

"father ciolek and i spent a lot of time planning everything."

"i'd like to say something, but i'm not reading from the bible."

"it's holy monday, james, father ciolek is doing us a favor by having your father's mass today, i told him you had to leave for california."

"i don't see how he's doing us any favors, i assume we're paying for the mass and for the hall."

"father is taking time out of the easter holiday rituals for your father."

"what time is he taking? he was going to do the mass anyway. god, all i'm asking for is a couple of minutes."

"father said no eulogies, it's still a holy monday mass."

"then i'm not reading."

"i told everyone you were."

"i don't care."

"i guess i shouldn't be surprised."

"i'm sorry, but i don't see how reading a bunch of words that a stranger picked out are somehow honoring dad at his memorial."

"that's all right, i'll read them myself."

she shuffles down the hall, into her room, into the soft lie of her head. a mothy robe around her, a loam of candlelights and morning lauds, primes, terces, little pleas she makes to god like the soft rain falling without a sound. she whispers into the backs of her eyes, around her rosary like the old christmas lights left on the gutters. i wonder if anyone is listening, but me. she is obvious to me and unknown, hidden even to herself and secretly satisfied that i've disappointed her. she only needed the old man to hurt her, now she needs me. jesus will love her no matter what, but what would a martyr be without their cross. her church is about suffering, her god is a jealous god. now she can be alone with him, her heartache on the long hem of her dress, the lamb laid down and toothless. she tells herself it's okay. it's okay, the same pattern her mother wore.

the morning is just under the ground. it's not light, but there is a promise of light, something behind the trees and above them, a feeling growing out of the east. the rain has bled the colors away and made everything gray like a black and white photo that is neither black nor white. everything seems to be coming from the space between the earth and the sky, the paradox of light, something turned to shade with just a hand and nothing to even touch.

i put my arms thru his slicker and step outside onto the porch, into his muck boots and the mist. the rain feels good on my face, on the tops of my eyes and my hands. by the time i get to the near bridge it will be light enough to see and between the trees. the sound of my steps on the gravel reminding me i'm not gone or a ghost yet or even dreaming. i could never dream this.

the weeds along the path seem taller since yesterday, wet with the new rain, reaching out and soaking my pants.

the long spade is where i left it, stuck in the ground, his maddox and his spud bar leaned against a tree, the mound like something found, like a dollar bill on the sidewalk or a five, something that makes you look around before you look down at it. it seems it's the first time i've seen it. i curl my tongue out and bite down, following its line up from the oak where it starts or maybe ends and off the rock ledge to where it rises from the ground again on the other side of the river, a large stone and another, small stones and clay. i'm alone in this thicket and mist, standing up with the trees, like another tree, like i could disappear into the woods. i have no sense of him, of nik, they're gone or gone on to something else.

this is the last day, my first days here in twelve years. i am fatherless, a clean space on the carpet where his chair sat, his hands under ten hundred stones, the rest of him dust in a box, the river running in its direction. i don't know if i'll come here again except to burn what's left of her and to throw her amongst the weeds. maybe i'll burn the house like he said or leave it for the river to take some rainy year if it can reach. all of it some damn husk of him, the lees at the bottom of his bottles, the skin rubbed off my shins and at my knees, all this sediment of us like the sawdust next to the saw. the old man told me once that everything is made of the same hundred elements, that you can destroy something, but you can never destroy what it's made of, that everything eventually becomes something else. i wonder where he is now and where nikki is sleeping, if the parrots from the square followed her and still keep her awake. i wonder what broke us apart and what will become of these pieces of us. the old man said no atom is ever lost or wasted, but no one really knows for sure.

i can hear burgermeister's truck on the gravel road, on the cement of the near bridge and back on the gravel again, the boil of his tires fading toward the house, it's almost eight. the road is relatively dry, the old rains still in the hollows. she's in the house painting on a strong face, still picking out a hat, singing in the mirror, rehearsing her special song for the old man, something he never heard. i start up the path past the prickers' git and stick, thru the new grass, his old tools worn sure at the handles where he held them, the grooves in my hands the same as his. i stop a moment and listen to the river, looking back across the mound weaving thru the woods and across the water. this is the end of them, where the work ends, nikki and the old man. it will become art if someone says so, otherwise it will come and go like a tree growing deep in a wood, in a dream, and extraordinarily unseen. it won't last, nothing but our memories do and even our memories stop i suppose. everything falls to the ground and to atoms and finally to a kind of nothing like the old man said. everything becomes something else.

25

town is two roads, where the river road turns to a street and church street, what makes four corners where they cross. it is earth, but of the water, a peninsula, the old man said an alluvial plain. nothing has changed except for a small strip of new stores, a video store and a drug store, a small gift shop filled with things you wouldn't want yourself, but buy to give away, a real estate office with photos in the window, "charming originals" and "custom lakefront homes". what was the donut shop, a counter and black coffee, is a leather boothed bar and grill now, brass fixtures and satellite television, someplace for the summer people. the townies drink at the townhouse, where our fathers drank and theirs, an old gravel parking lot and a red neon budweiser sign, a mid seventies monte carlo, primer and bondo, parked in front from last night or even the night before. everything in the rain the same as my memory, everything brick and wood and white paint, the red brick store and the old town hall, the sheriff's station next to it like a squat dog, the town square in the middle where it should be, green and treed, a cannon on the lawn pointed at the post office across the street. the old gas station is a b.p. now, four new pumps in front and a canopy. i remember when there was one pump, when there was nothing above, but the weather. behind the garage is a long dock and a shed house and an older dulled pump for the boats that seems to have always been there. the original standard oil sign still up like they couldn't give in to the british and take it down, the b.p. sign on the other corner, slightly shorter like a foreign flag.

burgermeister pulls to the side of the street, his truck too big for the church parking lot. the windshield wipers rubbing noisily now that we've stopped.

"i'm gonna let you off here mrs. tully."
"thank you tim, once again sweetheart saved the day."
"mom, can you get down from here?"
"i'm fine, tim showed me the trick."
"yeah man, check her out."
"burgermeister, get out and help her down."
"she's fine."

"i'm fine, james, see."

"jesus christ... just be careful please, i've had enough drama this week."

i follow after her, my suit pants at the point of tearing as i stretch down from the door, my foot searching for the curb.

"put your foot on the back tire first, like i did."

"whatever, mom, i'll get down my own way."

"don't tear your good pants."

"yeah, don't tear your fancy pants there, jimmy."

"it's james... fucking idiot."

i say "fucking idiot" under my breath, but our eyes met, he knew what i meant if he didn't hear me. it's good to be in the rain again, out of the truck, out from the smell of his wet jacket and her perfume, of his smoked cigarettes in the ashtray and the defroster, the trap of her hairspray hair. i sat between them on the bench seat, my knees against the stick shift. she had to have air, the window cracked, talking across me all the way to town, town gossip and church natter, blather of the weather and a girl named phyllis. it's good to be in town, to be stopped and quiet, if only for these moments between the rain and the church doors.

saint joseph's is at the end of town and the end of the old man somehow. everything tall grass past it to the lake, thrown out things and had it, land that will be built on someday if the church decides to sell it, weeds otherwise or winter snow drifts against a rolled out row of snow fence. the church building is brick simple, stained glass and stone steepled, the steps up to the wood doors quaried and peopled with men in blue suits and brown suits, the women in long coats and longer department store dresses, one hundred black umbrellas, a church bell once, it's a quarter to nine.

"james, oh my god will you look at everyone."
"yeah mom."
"your father was very well respected."
"i think they're here for you, mom."
"i can't believe everyone made it... by the grace of god."
"the wood bridge seemed okay, i suppose we could have drove ourselves."

we walk towards the church under the same umbrella, neither one of us keeping dry, but it's not raining hard enough to bother, burgermeister in the truck still, smoking a cigarette and picking at his zits in the rear view mirror. a hundred looks have turned to face us, faces drawn with straight lines and circles, old stories under umbrellas, hatted or dark scarved, table-legged women and wire-thin men, fat men and washed out women, colorless and part of the weather. their faces fall like the rain off my eyelashes

and shoulders, down the backs of our jackets, collecting
on the top of her hat. they part like a used bookstore book
folds open, waiting for us to walk between them despite
the drizzle.

"hello, good morning, good morning, yes, thank you, hello... james, we're sitting in front, dear."
"okay."
"good morning, thank you for coming, frank i'm so glad
you're here, ben would be so pleased, hello carl, hello,
yes thank you, god bless you... james, judy is going to sit
with us."
"that's fine, mom."
"thank you, yes, yes he was veronica's brother, yes thank
you, good morning mrs. janowicsz, yes martin and julia
are still alive, they should be here, hello, thank you, good
morning... james dear, i want to light some candles at the
holy mother's altar."
"do whatever you need to do, mom."
"don't you want to light a candle? i brought change for
you."
"go ahead, i'm going to get our seats."
"mrs. wyszniski you're so sweet to come, mary ellen, thank
you for coming, ann, ann over here! i'm fine don't worry..."

it's her moment and how i'll remember her until i won't
remember if she ever stood up straight. it's her alone, her
little glass feet, her husband's ashes in a black plastic can,

her only son merely a name, whispers amongst the town faces, "that's him, james". the faces tell me they're sorry. i nod and say thank you, but i'm really just watching, watching her grow bigger and bigger until she becomes a monument, watching her try on her crown of thorns. tomorrow will be different, the faces will go about their daily business and only pity her on sundays after mass in their kitchens when her name comes up and go back to eating their butterscotch puddings again. she will become part of the townies' papery talk, in the market and after choir practice, the old lady who smells funny and sits alone in church, her lips moving as if she's praying, talking to herself as if someone is listening, a lean cuisine and a cabbage and a can of cat food in her shopping cart. and she will become smaller and smaller until she is only a past, until we can't see her without thinking of when.

i step inside the vestibule, holy water out of habit, the father and the son and the holy spirit. two old men hold the inner doors open, their skin hung to their hanger bones, wet coats and umbrellas in the closet. they look at me like they know, like they brought on this death themselves like they bring the collection baskets before the eucharist. the church pews are dark wood and rowed and worn smooth, the ceiling as high as a sky, painted panels of flat saintly faces staring down at us, long byzantine faces lit with halos. the town faces are in their seats, their stares down to their knees, only looking where they've been and where they'll be. faces worn soft from factory work and fields, full faces and flushed cheeks, promises of big asses. this town is czechs and pollocks, irish and italians, peoples who eat, the jesus hanging behind the altar starved down to his strings, nearly naked and tortured. i can't look, i can only look at his feet like i'd look away from some strung out homeless soul in a doorway in the tenderloin, someone you give a dollar to before he even asks, hoping he doesn't ask so you don't have to see his eyes or let him see yours.

the church quiet is of whispers and the wisps of wet shoes on the carpet runner, on the terrazzo, a stifled cough, a man just behind me clearing his throat, two old women shuffling thru their purses for a handkerchief. it is the echo of our nightly prayers, the egg shell of our desperation, something in our heads, the buckshot of our shot out souls. when the pipe organ begins, mass will begin, the whispers hushed, when the bells have rang nine times...

"i can't believe the turnout, god has been so good to us... james, did you meet judy yet?"
"no."
"judy, this is james, my son."
"hi, it's nice to meet you."
the bell sounds, all of us looking up as if there was something to see.

"it's so nice to meet you finally, your mother tells me you're quite the artist."
"she tends to exaggerate."
"i'm sure you're very talented."

the bell sounds...

"james, that's theresa and the boys, brett and chuck."

i nod hello, judy and my mother sitting between me and them. they lean forward and smile like tourists that don't speak the language. all i'll remember is brett's or chuck's sparse mustache, i'll never know which one was which. one of them eighteen maybe and a man somehow, the other trying to be anything but fourteen, acned and short for his age. the woman not even gray, but like the rain and invisible except for her makeup, her lipstick a shade of red with an exotic name and as common as her best dress from the kmart two exits up from the river road off the highway.

the bell sounds...

"james we're so blessed, everything looks so beautiful, don't you think?"
"everything looks pretty much like i remember it."

"i mean the flowers and all the easter fanfare."

the bell sounds...

"they're really nice, mom."
"i guess not much changes around here."
"probably not."

the bell sounds...

"do i look okay."
"you look great, mom."
"i'm so nervous."

the bell sounds...

"you sing every sunday, you'll be fine."
"i wish your father would have heard me sing... just once, i'll never have that."
"maybe he will now."

the bell sounds...

"you're such a dear, james, of course he will, thank you."

the bell sounds...

"your father loved you, despite the disease, he loved you."

the bell sounds...

we wait. we know their rhythm now like a part of our pulse, but it is the end. we look up again, not as if we'd seen something, but as if we'd lost something instead, the ring still in our ears as it dies away in the air, all of us always trying to hold on, a death we expected and listened for and were surprised by still, only the bell keeper keeping count. the organ begins in one rush of blood, a red faced priest in a white robe and gold amice walking in from the back, walking up the center aisle not so much like a man who sees god, but like a man who's looking. two altar boys in front of him and two behind, a crucifix and a chalice at the ends of their arms, a paten and piscina, careful steps onto the predella.

the world is ten thousand things and a secret, christ's secret in the ambry behind the altar, bits of bread and wine that will become body and blood by the end of mass, by the evocation of a man in new shoes, by the silence of latin, something almost sung if not spoken, a thick of incense, a resin of frankincense and sadness, a barefoot jesus above him. she'll rise and sing a song with the choir behind her, i'll only hear her, i won't listen, the bells still in my head, the memory of car tires on the gravel road, nikki crying on the phone, trying to remember the timbre of the old man's voice. and she'll read between the dreaming of the father's latin and his holy communion and i'll listen to the last words as if i was supposed to.

"...therefore if any man be in christ, he is a new creature, old things are passed away, behold, all things are become new, this is the word of the lord."

i don't know the words, but i've somehow always known them, something the old man said. i'll read them again, corinthians, in the daily mass program the old church men handed out at the door. and i will fold them and put them in my suit pocket and find them years later and remember the words without even reading them and hang them back in the closet and wear a different jacket.

the faces will take of christ's body and his blood and be new again like corinthians said, like the river after a heavy rain, but i believe in water more than wine. the father will repeat the latin that was repeated to him and the faces will respond "praise be to god" and "amen" and the organ will bleed again till everything is red, the choir and the stained glass, the madonna and the old women's lipsticked lips, the town faces in their seats waiting for us to rise and leave.

she's bent over crying like she's just discovered he's dead. her friends helping her up, helping her down the aisle. i can only walk behind her and make up her myth. someday the truth won't matter, it hardly matters now, the river running to the lake regardless of our stories. it's raining still.

the bell sounds...

we look up and don't know why.

26

it's just her now, what was her and him, a son between them, somehow the two of us hunched under an umbrella. the old man, he went and did it and died wednesday night, thursday early morning really, his body finally listening to what he'd been shouting all these years. what he left us won't fit in a sample jar or show on an x-ray, but we'll show symptoms all the same, his last name painted on the mail box. i can't help, but to think what became new of him and where we're all going, me hobbling along, my atoms spiraling around something i guess. she's still a young woman some women would say, an old woman and more broken than me, maybe a mother, the best she could be, a weed grown out of her mother's rose garden.

the reception hall is across the parking lot from the church, new brick and seventies ugly, cheap cinder block and flat roofed. the floor given to green vinyl tiles, the ceiling, a drop ceiling, the panels water stained brown in places, traces of past leaks and gray circles where they're wet now, flat roofs never work. the hall's smell is the color of its paint, an institutional white that's neither white nor yellow, the smell of school rooms and government offices, a residue of detentions and waiting in line. there is an open space that is meant to be a dance floor in front of a stage, a plywood platform two steps up and a microphone, the rest of the room metal folding chairs and long folding tables covered with red plastic table cloths left over from christmas.

the faces are filing in the glass double doors, hanging up their jackets on the coat racks in the foyer, looking for food like loose dogs, lining up at the bar, ginger ale and whiskey, whiskey and seven up, drinks that old men drink. the men standing around with their ties loosened and their big brown shoes, their shoulders back like they might say something. the women talking in tight circles, big women like warm pies, their hips pried wide apart by nine and ten pound babies, big boned and sturdy, their children grown and taller than them.

"james, john kapelka wants to talk to you."

"about what?"

"i don't know, dear. i saw him at the virgin's altar and he told me that he needed to have a word with you after mass."

"i don't know why he'd need to talk to me."

"all he said was he had to talk to you."

"maybe it's about the insurance."

"i don't know, dear."

"it has to be the car... i don't know what else it would be."

"james dear, can you help roseanne with the food, tom's taking off work to help kathy with everything, but poor roseanne's on her own."

"where is she? "

"i saw her in the parking lot... here she is, roseanne! james is going to help you."

"hi, i'm james tully."

"nice to meet you, can you take this?"

"oh yeah, absolutely, sorry."

"just set it over there, there's more in the front room and in the car, i can't carry it all."

"just tell me what you need me to do."

"come on then, the food's getting cold."

"sorry."

"are you paying me, because i need another fifty dollars, everything wound up being more than i expected."

"um, my mom's paying i guess, i didn't know i... i only have sixty cash on me."

"never mind, here, take these pig's feet and the dumplings over to the table."

"okay... wow they're heavy."

"there's more pig's feet in the trunk, i made a hundred, your mother wanted everyone to have one."

"how can you eat just one?"

"what?"

"nothing."

"you can help me with what's in the car, i can carry the sauerkraut."

she's a squat lady, a stump maybe of a taller woman once, worn down from the work, from the working man she married and the children that broke her water. she's a long face and cross black shoes, breasts that are almost her entire body and a nuisance now if they were ever anything else. we set the large metal pans of "authentic czech food" on a long table off to the side of the other tables, just outside of an empty kitchen.

"is this going to be okay, ma'am?"

"as long as people can reach it."

"oh roseanne! everything looks wonderful, just wonderful."

"i'm going to need another fifty dollars, the pigs feet were more than i thought."

"of course, that's fine roseanne, just tell me how much you need."

"i just did."

"yes, well i'll have james add it up, i don't trust myself with the math."

"i'll come and pick up the pans at noon."

"i was hoping you'd stay, eddie and carl are playing."

"i'll be back at noon."

"well thank you for everything. james, don't you think everything just looks amazing?"

"yeah mom, i've never seen anything like it."

"i'd appreciate if the pans are clean when i come back."

"certainly, roseanne."

"mr. tully i'll meet you at the car."

"what was that all about?"

"oh she's just upset because i asked kathy to make the corned beef and cabbage."

"jesus, what a bitch."

"oh don't mind her."

"mom, i'd like to say something."

"go ahead dear, you know you can always talk to me."

"i mean i want to say something about dad, i've been thinking about it for a couple of days."

"father ciolek is eulogizing your father after everyone has eaten, he's coming over for pork feet and dumplings in a few minutes, we talked about it yesterday."

"this guy didn't even know dad."

"that's not true, i told you your father made strudel

for father every apple season, he knows all about your
father."

"he might know all about him, but he doesn't know
him."

"i don't understand what you're saying."

"what i'm saying is all these people stuffing their faces
don't even know dad, they only know what you told them."

"that's not true, frank stuckley has known your father since
he was six."

"that's one person."

"janice, frank's wife, has known your father as far back
as case, she met frank at school. and your aunt and uncle
are here, of course your aunt veronica passed away four
years come christmas, she's not here, but your cousins all
made it. they all know your father."

"okay, there's people here that knew dad... my point is i
want people to... i don't know... to hear something good
about him."

the band starts, stopping everything else like a punch
line to a dirty joke, something loud and inappropriate,
an accordion and a saxophone, a polka like every polka,
up and down and across like a plaid. the faces bob along
with the music, already with their paper plates in hand,
their plastic forks and knives rolled in a paper napkin, their
drinks finished, but for the ice, back at the bar waiting

for ray and their second or third, their wives saving their
places in line.

"what did you say? dear."

"you know what mom, forget it, anything i'd say would
just be wasted on these people anyway. they'll all be drunk
before we even get the rest of the food out."

"your father wanted us to celebrate his life not his death."

"i doubt dad wanted any of this."

"he did, we talked about it."

"whatever."

"well, i'm telling you he did."

"it doesn't matter."

"james, people are eating and the band is starting, why
don't you get a plate of food, you must be starving. you're
not going to get food like this in california."

"i don't think they'd allow it across the state line."

"this is where you're from, like it or not."

"most of it i wish i could forget."

"don't be that way, please james."

"all i wanted was to say a few things about dad."

"i don't want to interrupt eddie and the band while
they're playing. they're doing us a favor, they're playing
for half their regular rate because your father was such
a loyal fan."

"heaven forbid i interrupt eddie and carl, christ sake mom,

it's ten a.m. monday morning, what the hell else are they
going to do."

"the polka dots are very popular here, they're booked
constantly."

"bullshit."

"please james don't be harsh with me, i spent a lot of time
planning this, i just want things to go smoothly. what if you
say your eulogy at the ash spreading ceremony?"

"ash spreading ceremony?"

"i asked father ciolek to be there and i invited my support group from alanon and my prayer group from saint
joseph's. don't say anything to your aunt or uncle, i didn't
invite any of your father's family, the memorial is enough.
i can only take so much of them."

"jesus mom, i was hoping we could keep it simple, do we
have to have all these people?... the hell with it, you know
what, do what you want, you're going to anyway."

"where are you going?"

"i have to help that crazy woman bring the rest of the
food in if you can call it that."

i turn and walk thru the faces, old faces i knew when i was
young, faces that seemed always old. everyone i can only
squint at and remember and not really see, seeing what's
been put on and taken away and nothing else.

"jimmy, how ya holdin' up?"

"jimmy dear, you look so thin, has that wife of yours been feeding you?"

an uncle and an aunt and a gravel of cousins looking more worn than they should, but life is hard here, cigarettes and brown liquor, second shifts and cold weather.

"uhmm, i've got to help bring in the food, uhmm... i'll be back in a second... it's good to see you..."

it's the kind of thing you say as you're walking away, with nothing really to say, but a weak smile. and her with a weak smile anyway and him with his hand around his third seven and seven and a soggy paper napkin stuck to the sides.

the other faces, the church goers and the townies, stare at me like i've committed a lewd act, what they can't cop to watching and can't look away from. they are the faces of my dreams, strangers i thought i made up, what i recognize now and as anonymous in their shoes as they are in my sleep so i don't know if i'm awake. all of them at the makeshift buffet or already eating, pig's feet and sauerkraut, dumplings in salted pork grease. the other table like the other side of a war, corned beef and cabbage and boiled potatoes. my aunt julia like a wrung out rag, her skin too big for her bones, off at her own table standing over a stock pot, ladling out heaps of the gelatinous carp and ginger snaps and prunes only the old czechs will eat, the old family recipe, grandma said bohemian, everyone else said czech.

the old people look like they haven't eaten all day, but they have, drip coffee from the can, old wax paper wrapped bread, toasted so you'd never know it's stale, cheap cookies from the bag. they've been waiting though, they knew they'd eat good today, ben tully, priscilla's husband, passed away. all of them with their cauliflowered faces, waiting in their green cloth upholstered chairs, in their dark rooms, in their greasy yellow kitchens, yellow tiles and tiles missing, always yellow and light blue tiles too, something of '36 or '37 when everything was rebuilt.

"james tully, you're not going to have carp?"
"hi, aunt julia."
"we haven't seen you in a long time, i guess you're a real california boy now. you even remember the rain anymore?"
"i live in san francisco, aunt julia, it actually rains a lot."
"really, well who knew... well my carp might not be as good as your father's was, but i've been cooking since saturday."
"i'm sure it's every bit as good as my dad's."
"go get yourself a plate."
"i'll have to come back and get some, i have to go help my mom's friend with the rest of the food."
"i'll make sure to save some for you, i made it for the family."

"thanks, aunt julia."

i walk away with the word 'family' awkwardly in my arms, a notion i can't seem to hold or carry. regardless of its start, my blood seems mine, the rain turns to something else once it's fallen.

i make my way thru the hall past the peoples, past their coats hanging in the foyer like a line of past lives i've lived thru, thinking of all the coats i've worn and the women, nikki and dana, tracy and lori, the lonely of their empty closets once they'd gone, the nothingness now somehow more than the clutter, clothes on lavender hangers once, their shoes strewn across the floor.

"that's the last of the pig's feet, i'll be back at noon, please have the pans clean."
"sure, thanks."

she closes the car door and disappears into the seat of an old montero, her head barely above the wheel and well below the seat back. the winters and road salt have almost taken the wheel wells and the fenders, the steel becoming something else like everything else. the car pulls away leaving me alone in the parking lot with two large pans of pig's feet stacked on top of each other, the blue smoke of burnt oil and gas exhaust turning to acid in the rain at my ankles.

"let me carry those and you take your father's ashes."
"kapelka."
"how are you, james."
"i'm good..."

we look at each other like men will and start to laugh, the kind of laugh that is a man's only alternative to crying. we can't stop to say what has to be said, what might not need to be said anymore. the two of us standing in a crescent of rain, a drizzle we've grown immune to, holding trays of pig's feet and my father's remains, carrying a dark madness that has finally caught up with us, something indigenous to the peoples of the great lakes, wakes and midwest parking lots.

"james, i need to talk to you about your father."

the laughing stops.

"what?"
"well after everything that happened with your father's body..."
"kapelka... please, i had a good reason, i'm... i don't know...

even if he was a drunk he was my root, he's all i really had. i did what i did because i loved him..."

"james, i don't doubt that you loved your father, i..."

"remember what you said about people doing things, you know crazy things sometimes when they're under stress... i had to bring him into the cellar by myself."

"james, believe me i appreciate how hard this weekend must have been on you, my brother and i talked this morning, he and i are partners at the mortuary, considering everything that went on..."

"come on, jesus, you know better than anyone how fucking crazy it was out there that night."

"james, we'd like to pay for the cremation."

"what?"

"i know it's meaningless in comparison to what happened, but it's all i can think of to try to make things right. i feel like i let you and your family down, you have every right to file a grievance with the state mortuary..."

"wait a minute, you're afraid i'm going to turn you in?"

"i hope you'll consider the set of circumstances i was facing... i hope you can forgive me."

"that's what you wanted to talk to me about?"

"yes."

i start to laugh again, bent over with the effort, reckless with relief. i set the pans down and take a pig's foot out from under the aluminum foil that covers them, kapelka turning his head at me like a dog might. i toss it up into the air catching it in my hand and then rear back and throw the foot at a tree amongst a woods behind the parking lot, hitting it square in the middle of its trunk, the pig's foot falling to pieces into the weeds. kapelka looks at me in disbelief and then laughs himself, maybe with me or at me or at the world we're wrapped in like the last fifty pigs feet in two pans. i hand him a foot like the start of some sunday school prank or a saturday act of contrition, forgive me father for i have sinned and it's been... since my last confession. he awkwardly teeters and almost stumbles and throws it, missing, but satisfied, the both of us laughing like we don't know about dying, but kapelka knows, he knows all about death and me with my father's ashes at the ends of my arms.

we walk back into the hall together, kapelka carrying in the pig's feet like a kill, me with some part of myself in a can, smiling still if not laughing and laughing sadly at the polka dots playing something ridiculous, like she says the old man wanted. all the old czechs have drank up their drinks, some still with drinks in their hands, dancing in their old way circles, some secret told and forgotten. all the women and their thick hosed ankles, their square heeled black shoes, their husbands with old eyes and old football ears, red veined noses and gray hair just over their spotted scalps.

"jesus christ, the corned beef is gone."

"there's plenty of pig's feet."

"i haven't had a decent thing to eat in four days."

"they don't look too bad."

"are you going to eat one?"

"no."

"james dear, isn't the food just wonderful."

"i don't know mom i haven't ate anything yet and now there's nothing left."

"why didn't you eat?"

"because i was outside bringing in the rest of the stupid pig's feet."

"your grandmother loved them."

"christ these people went thru the corned beef like they hadn't seen food for a week."

"i'm sure your aunt julia saved you some carp."

"god this can't be happening, i just want some real food."

"don't let roseanne hear you saying that, thank god she wasn't here to see kathy's corned beef go like it did... is that your father?"

"i guess."

"i can't believe we're really here, forty two years...my darling ben."

she takes the canister away from me and into her arms like a birthday present, a look on her face that has no meaning between the living.

"are you okay?"

"i'm fine, like i said we're here to celebrate your father's life not his death. you eat james, i'm going to dance."

she drifts onto the dance floor like a fallen leaf in a current, the container of my father's ashes in her arms. but where are any of us, but in the current of our fates or god's will or dumb luck.

"hell with it... kapelka can you give me a ride to the diner? i'm not eating this shit."

"i would, but it won't do you any good, carolanne is sitting over there to the left and there's nothing else open, the donut shop's a fancy restaurant now and they're not open on mondays."

"will you take me home then, i need to get out of here."

"what about your mother."

"look at her she's fine, she's dancing, talking with her friends."

"james, it's not my place to tell you how to honor your father's passing, but don't you think you'll regret leaving?"

"no, my father would have hated this."

"well if you want to go home i'll take you, it's your decision, it's the least i can do."

"give me a minute."

the accordion breathes in and out, the saxophone just out

as they dance, all of them like the buffet had depended on it, everything gone, but the pigs feet and the stock pot of my aunt julia's carp sitting alone like the fat girl at the class social.

"mom, john kapelka is going to take me home."
"dear, what's wrong?"
"i don't know, i just want to go home."
"you're so much like your father, james. go ahead, i'll be home by one and we'll spread your father's ashes like we talked about, okay."
"okay... thanks mom... i'm sorry."
"don't be sorry, dear, i understand. you and your father are your own men, he loved the music, but at a certain point he'd always say he'd had enough of the crowds and we'd go home. i loved him, james, despite everything, i loved him."
"i know."
"i love you, you know that."
"i love you too, mom, i'll see you at the house."

i can feel myself starting to cry, but i push it back into the back of my throat, someplace black behind where they took my tonsils out, somewhere even secret to me, a cistern of tears that will never leave me, tears i'll cry some other time for some other reason, but they will be her tears and his, water welled deep from years of rains. i motion to kapelka who has been watching us, still standing next to the trays of pigs feet like he were presenting an open casket. i walk to the door, wading thru the faces dancing in their flower print dresses, in their j.c. penney suits, let out pants that fit in the seventies, lapels that are a bit too wide like their feet, the beat of the accordion. i turn back to look for kapelka and see my mother dancing alone inside her hat, an empty space around her, stopping and turning and almost whirling and not even crying, only smiling a strange smile that seems fixed to her like she was dead herself. my mother was my father's wife.

27

while the townies talk of the weather, the weather knocks down trees, in the end it's what we do that matters. kapelka is talking about the rain, about the river flooding, something to fill the time in and finally nothing, but the long silence of the hearse's tires, what comes last, i guess. i've heard him, but i haven't listened, my attention at the water running across the rolled up window and at the bare trees past that. the old man never talked much, he'd say, a man is what a man does, and go on doing what he did. he went to the river like that, like a rain and to the great lake. he worked every day.

i asked him once what was at the bottom of the lake, once, when he was gathering samples, letting out the long lines he used to catch catfish, the two of us in the old aluminum boat. he told me that there was most likely water there, but he didn't know for sure, that most of life is believing and never knowing. he said that the only remedy for faith is work, that the only way to know something was to do something.

i can't know the truth, but i've done my best to tell it. i can't even know what happened, i only know when and where and where i am now, the river road and the river, the portion west to the lake. for her it won't matter, she'll make something up and keep it with her keepsakes. everything in the dusty shadow box the old man made her, what he did back when they were first married and he could still cut a straight line. nikki will tell her next man about me like she knew me and never know herself, humming along to an old song on the radio and not singing the words. what it all meant is water now, what runs underground, something we have to find for ourselves, by ourselves. no well is deeper than the center of our bones.

the house is around me and surely lodged in my lungs, the late afternoon shadows, the spaces where he was and where she left us, the last stone in place. the rain has stopped and maybe even the air, there is nothing, but the heat again, but the fan upstairs, but my matter and mass. everything pulling at the past and the past pulling at me, spilt candle wax and all their promises in the cracks between the floor boards and the stains on the carpets, the broken screen door hanging on in the back, his suicide in the cabinet under the counter. the grout between the small tiles in the bathroom is crumbling, some tiles are loose and some tiles are gone completely. the bathroom tub is ringed with the river and their oil, my old room, older and plaster cracked, painted over, but unchanged.

i haven't bothered to shave for days, i need something between then and now. i've showered and put on clean clothes, but a matter of the river and the river clay soughs from my skin still, just below the smell of yellow soap. i wonder if i'll ever get this place out from under my nails. i'm sitting on my old bed looking down at my hands, looking thru the small windows at the trees, the thin mattress and the bed springs curving beneath me like an old woman's back might break. i stick out my tongue and run its muscle along the rough edges of my teeth. i sit and listen to the fan, listening for the stew of tires on the gravel road, the click of the front door, her bunion feet, it's almost four, the oven clock says three-twenty-two, she should have been home hours ago.

i was eighteen when i left here. the old man gave me his ford knowing my old datsun would never make it. he told me he should have known better, that both my grandfathers were u.a.w., that they'd roll over in their graves if they knew i drove anything but an american car. he knew i'd never come back, i don't know if he knew i'd never really leave. he came up from the river and met me at the near bridge as i was driving away. he leaned in the window and hugged me goodbye, we both seemed surprised. he smelled of work, of the river and cigarettes, maybe whiskey. the same smell when he carried me out of the river, my wet hair pressed against his chest then, my chin well above his shoulder by now. he started back to the river, but he stopped and turned and he looked right at me. he said that the great lakes were the biggest lakes in the world, but that the smallest hand could move them, that he'd never seen an ocean, but he suspected the pacific was no different. he almost smiled and he turned and walked back down the ravine until i couldn't see him, until all i would see was the tops of the trees.

i've put the house key above the back door, my bag in the back seat of the rental. i can't wait for her, for his ashes and atoms, my plane is in three hours. i look over at the merc, it's the first thing she'll see, its front doors wide open, a mound of rock and river clay running out of the ground and across the big front bench seat, what i built while i was waiting for her. burgermeister will say "what the fuck?" and go on about how i don't have any common sense and think hard on how he can part out the old man's car. she'll go in the front door, he always used the back, he said the front door was for salesman and company. she'll utter some little prayer like she's breathing and make a sign of the cross and walk past the space where his chair was, a mound of rocks and whiskey bottles now. she'll be calling for me, she won't have noticed that the rental car is gone. she won't understand where i could be, her husband's ashes in her arms. she'll put the black plastic container of him on the kitchen table with the leftover pigs' feet she couldn't give away and my aunt julia's carp. a fitting memorial in front of his chair, his kitchen chair stacked with rocks and a gas station giveaway glass.

i'm on the gravel road winding thru the woods like a secret passed thru the saint joseph's ladies group, something everybody knows anyway, the old house and the river road at the gravel road's two ends. i suppose it was the easiest route when my grandfather cut it, folks were close to the earth then. it's dry enough for the rental, though the road is rutted from times of rain and a history of cars and trucks, from years of the merc and her camaro, the old man's pick up, from burgermeister's truck these last few days. it is cut deep and yet it is a good road and somehow mine more than anything i know.

i stop at the near bridge and look up the river to the rock ledge. you can see the end of the mound i built there or the beginning, there's no telling where things really start or stop. no one will look, she'll never see it. his hands another mystery of bones and artifacts, arrowheads and tie tacks. i don't know where it all started, any of us, me or him, the indians or the river, but in the end we are all the same thing. this is the end and the end is always sad.

i've made the river road, everything suddenly quiet, only the thick air in the windows and a hum of tires instead of the splatter of the gravel and mud in the wheel wells. the water is around the trees, the river road built up and high enough to the east to be dry. i'm there again, away from here again, away from the house and them, but this is as far as i'm going to get regardless of where i go.

she'll be home by four thirty, she'll say it wasn't quite three. she'll have a story, she always had a story. i'll be getting gas at the gas station town halfway when she calls, i won't have a signal, i won't get her message until i'm north on the highway. i'll call her back, but the line will be busy. she'll be on the phone all evening. she'll call her friend judy from saint joseph's and then the others, mary beth and maria, theresa and ann, evelyn and loretta. she'll tell them how great it was to have "james home". she'll talk about "james's sculptures" like they're not hers, like the house and what happened here was somebody else. they'll talk about how beautiful the mass and the memorial were and god bless and goodnight. she'll think to make tea and drink warm water from the tap instead, she'll forget to

put the leftovers away and remember to pray and sleep in
her wrinkled bed with all her teeth in her head as if they
were in a drawer.

i can hear the river from the gas station pump, from the
small grocery and hardware that are the town halfway to
the highway. everything is stopped like it does before a
rain starts, before the sky breaks like an ankle. i follow the
sound or not even the sound, but a feeling you get, a sense
of something to the back of the garage to take a last look
at the river. somehow i know it's there. there are tires and
rusted car parts, a sign that says "sold", oil filters and fan
belts worn to fibers, beer bottles scattered all about my
feet, feathers from birds, things i'm not sure what we do
with or how we do without. and there is the sound of the
river, but there is only the woods and the weeds and the
remains of what we left and what we lost, a muddy path
that goes on and on.

i start down a part in the weeds behind the garage to the
river and stop when it turns steep. there is only a crease in
the trees where the path was and trees after that and no
worn way that i can see. i turn around, my tongue pushed
between my teeth, my steps pressed into the mud the same
way there as back, back to the rental car at one of the two
pumps waiting like a bad blind date.

there's a greasy puddle in a dip in the black top next to
the white cinder block garage, motor oil pearled on top
of the left over rain. i can see myself and the bruise of
the sky above me, everything behind me reflected back,
when the water is still, when i am still. i hold my breath
and look, sometimes i'd rather think of nik than breathe,
what she left of me rippled in the water. the old man told
me once, if you're going to drown yourself, there's no use
wading in shallow water. he never seemed to have a choice,
he never learned to swim.

there is a certain sadness welded to any bit of acceptance,
an end if not a resolve. i'm not sure if letting go isn't just
the last gasp. there aren't many answers and maybe that's
all i'll know. i asked the old man if he was afraid of the
water. he almost laughed before he frowned and said that
he was only afraid of drowning. he went out into the river
after that and he turned back to me on the bank holding a
sample jar and said that the water would always be around
me, that it would pull me and push me, but to remember
that it's only around me, that it isn't about me. i knew
what he meant then, but i was young and close to the start,
close enough to see things without the blur of time and
experience. maybe as you get close to the end you can see
again. the old man, he seemed to know almost everything,
but he always knew he was going to die.

there seemed a river somewhere, something past the trees, but there's only me, or something of me, reflected in this puddle and in all of them, her and him, the blue blue eyes i stared in. this puddle will be nothing by summer, everything disappears into the ground. everything is of something else so it seems our lives and even our memories are just borrowed, what lives in us and dies with me. i will remember, i have to, and forget and live with it just the same, just beneath my skin. everything was nothing first.

in seventh grade science class they told us that the human body is made mostly of water, the old man said fifty seven to sixty three percent, even our bones. he always said it was hard to see things as they really are, that you can't see the river standing in it and you can't really know it anywhere else. we are water i believe. i am water, and water finds a way, softly around and eventually thru the rock.

acknowledgments

it takes a lifetime to write anything. to all of you who were a part or even a kindly passerby on this journey, on my kid street or the state route out, the long long desert road or the winding way up the mountain to here, you have my deepest gratitude.

my thanks: to liz dubelman and paul slansky for believing and making it a book. to andy summers for a north star to aim for. to chris moore and his heart of ten men. to ed solomon for an early ear that mattered. to cathy colman for letting out my ghosts. to dana stevens for her ever present hand on my shoulder. to jordan and joe levin for seeing when i said look. to joshua weinfeld and rob roberts for helping me make the road rhyme. to steven bergstrom, deane birkett and roy page for keeping my wheels rolling. to suzanne "cash" wright for something when there's nothing. to patti connolly and the irish we sing. to scott shellstrom for painting the picture. to david dearth, rest in peace, for this big west. to miki and kazuko morishita for a far east. to hannelore hutton for simply saving my life.

and to miwa and sorcha, you are the everything... luck is of the undeserving and i am the luckiest of all.

about the author

brian david cinadr has had his short stories published in the country's most prestigious liter- ary journals: The Alaska Quarterly, The Big Muddy, The South Dakota Review, The South Carolina Review, Soundings East, WaterStone, ZYZZYVA...  He is the recipient of Cal State Northridge's Best Short Fiction, 2003 and is a two time Pushcart Award nominee for America's Best Short Story.

born and raised in cleveland, ohio and based in the coastal mountains of southern california, brian has acquired a broad group of readers and supporters. his life is storied with strippers and studio executives, mafia businessmen and neighborhood pushers. he has had a career in body-building, dug graves, bodyguarded for a myriad of rock stars and hollywood celebrities. brian's stories grow out of his rust belt working roots, stories of his common folk, of the factories and the fields of his childhood, of the highways that gave him hope and a vague faith in god and an america that haunt him still.

https://briandavidcinadr.com/

Made in the USA
San Bernardino, CA
13 March 2020

65520159R00190